The [...] lmost exactly as Dure[...] een brutally beaten about the h[...] body. His jaw had been broken, his teeth smashed—and they clung in bloody, dark ivory fragments to his lips, like jagged froth. The hand that rested on his lap had been twisted, the wrist broken, the fingers bent back until they looked like shattered twigs, all at odd angles. The old man's eyes, sightless even in life, were open and his face turned upward, as the rain fell softly on the grotesque caricature of his battered fea-

[...] died hard. And with him had died Sam Durell's [...]pe of learning how and why the highest powers [...]rnational crime had suddenly turned their lethal [...] to international espionage . . .

Assignment • • • • •

PALERMO

EDWARD S. AARONS

A FAWCETT GOLD MEDAL BOOK

Fawcett Publications, Inc., Greenwich, Conn.

To

JACK DENTON SCOTT

THE OLD MAN leaned back and turned his blind, ravaged face anxiously to the warm sunlight. He spoke in a quiet voice to Durell. "If someone is determined enough, clever enough, and angry enough, and he wants to kill you, he shall succeed. Somewhere. Somehow. Sometime. The victim is doomed. He is a walking corpse."

Durell sat still in the soft wind that blew over the lake and listened to his death sentence.

"*Is* there someone like that?" the blind man asked after a small silence.

"Yes, sir."

"And he is determined?"

"Yes."

"Clever?"

"Very. Kronin is the very best they have."

"I do not know this Kronin. Is he angry?"

"He wants me out of it. I can't get out."

The old man's name was Colonel Mignon. Looking at him, Durell felt as if he were considering a myth, a living fable. He had come a long way to see him. Mignon hadn't been in the business for a long time, not since the acid hit his face and blinded him in Vienna in 1954. He had been allowed to retire, which was something not often permitted, and had lived in this villa ever since, among the mountains rearing up out of the Italian lakes that bordered the Swiss Ticino.

The wind stirred Durell's thick black hair, and he brushed it back, aware that he had more gray at his temples than before. The terrace was built of pink marble, adorned with Roman copies of Greek sculpture. Last night it had looked like a graveyard. Mignon had refused to see him. An overseas telephone call to No. 20 Annapolis Street, in Washington, D.C., had fixed that.

It was peaceful here. Like a calm before the storm, Durell thought. The fishing village below the terrace tumbled down to the steep shore of the lake in a helter-skelter pattern of red and yellow tiled roofs. Music sounded dimly from the restaurant built out over the water, where the small white lake steamers came from Lugano with their crowds of gawking tourists. Most of the tourists were German—women with fat bottoms and pot hats, the men following after in their waddling wake. Children played on the steps of the streets that twisted down between the bright stucco houses, and their cries, in Ticinese Italian, added to the irony of the peaceful scene.

"Colonel Mignon?"

The old man had fallen asleep. He wore large dark glasses with eccentric heavy rims to cover the damage done by the acid thrown in his face so many years ago. He looked frail, even skeletal, with wispy white hair and a hard, wide mouth like a trap. He wore a mouse-colored flannel robe, although the sun was hot and the wind was warm. Somewhere in the villa, two peasant women moved softly about to attend to him. There was a high stone fence surrounding the place, with an antique bronze door of enormous weight, and Durell had seen to it that the bolts were firmly slammed home when he arrived. There were medallions and mementos of the old Kingdom of Savoy painted in *trompe-l'oeil* on the pink facade of the villa.

"Colonel Mignon?" he said again.

Durell could not tell if the hooded eyes behind those enormous glasses were open or not. But the hard mouth opened and spoke.

"Yes, yes. There is a resolution of sorts."

Durell waited.

Mignon said, "You could hide. Indefinitely. For years. Not a pleasant prospect. Not for you, eh?"

"Even if I wanted to—"

"But you do not wish it."

6

"—I couldn't."

"So I understand. I heard your name on the radio. I understand it is in the newspapers." The old man clicked his tongue. *"Tchk!* You are not the sort of person, Mr. Durell, to get into a barroom brawl accidentally, after smashing a car on the promenade and arguing with the *agents,* and having yourself arrested for drunkenness, and spending the night in our local jail."

"I wasn't drunk," Durell said.

"I did not say you were. It was deliberate. I guessed this. You wish to attract attention, to let people know where you are. A very dangerous ploy, sir. Not too practical. You want to lure the killer into a trap?"

"Not yet. I had to do it for another reason. I'm looking for someone. Three people. They're somewhere in Switzerland, hiding out. I want them to know where I am so they'll come to me. I need them. I need their help. And I think they'll recognize me as a friend."

"So."

Durell said nothing more.

"And if the killer comes first? You trap him?"

"Not that, either. I need information first."

"I see. You take on an added risk. And, of course, delay the only other possible resolution. Fire with fire. You really should kill first."

"I intend to," Durell said quietly.

A butterfly alighted on the old man's gnarled hand and moved its wings slowly, dusty gold and black in the morning sunshine. There was laughter from the restaurant far down the hillside on the water's edge. The butterfly took off and settled on a potted oleander.

"The killer you mention," said Colonel Mignon, turning his blind eyes again toward Durell, "may make some mistakes. It is possible. We are all fallible. First he may send someone else to perform his errand. He may not try personally. This will be to your advantage because the hired man will not have his employer's incentive. Then, he may grow impatient. This, too, will help if he moves too soon. And his anger may make his brain

7

hot instead of cold. One must be very cold to kill properly."

"He has already made his greatest mistake," Durell said. "I know Kronin and I know his intentions."

The old man laughed. It was like a sound from the grave.

In Durell's business you learned to be very careful, always, if you hoped to survive. He was familiar with danger. He lived with it always, every minute, every day. But usually it was impersonal, and you weighed this factor against that and chose your course like a gambler calculating favorable odds. He had long ago learned to think this way from his old Grandpa Jonathan, back in Bayou Peche Rouge. Jonathan was one of the last of the old-time Mississippi riverboat gamblers. Danger and death were simply occupational hazards.

But this was different.

Durell was a tall, quiet man with a heavy musculature, a lean and weathered face, and dark blue eyes that turned black with thought or anger. He had learned to control his volatile Cajun temperament, and his years at Yale, studying law in New England, gave an overlay and quiet polish to his boyhood bayou character. Despite his height and size, he always moved with a lithe and easy grace. He could lose himself in a crowd when he wished, but another observer in the business would soon know him as a dangerous and effective man. He was a subchief in field operations for the trouble-shooting K Section of the Central Intelligence Agency. He knew that his survival factor had run perilously low since his first years in the old G-2, and all the later time when he went on into the CIA to work in the dark and silent war of unheralded violence in all the nameless corners of the world. He knew there were red-tabbed files on him at KGB headquarters in Moscow and in the P.L.I. security offices in Peiping, and in Hanoi and Prague. Nothing in those files promised him a long or peaceful life.

But Kronin was another matter.

Durell spoke a dozen languages fluently and could get along in another score of dialects. He had a gambler's hands, with strong, deft fingers, and he knew how to kill in a number of ways—with the edge of his palm, with stiffened fingers, a rolled newspaper, a long pin. He usually disdained the gimmicks dreamed up by the lab boys in the basement of K Section's headquarters on Annapolis Street in Washington. He knew the value of team work, but he preferred to work alone. Through the years he had come to accept the solitude of his work and he never turned a corner or opened a door without expecting the worst. It set him apart. There were times when he regretted this, but there was no turning back. Not now; not ever. It was his job, and he could see no other way of life for himself.

The blind old man coughed and huddled in his robe in the sunshine. A canary flickered like a drop of gold and alighted on one of the Roman statues adorning the terrace; it sang a brief note and departed.

"Mr. Durell," Colonel Mignon said, "you see what I have become. I am retired. You know your problem better than I. There is nothing I can do to help you. Even if I could, I would not. I have had enough. I want no more of it. You see, I was unlucky. I should have been killed. But here I am, with wasted black years."

"Do you regret your work, sir?" Durell asked.

The big dark glasses flashed in the sunlight as the skeletal head turned sharply toward him. "Now I only regret living. I'm out of it for good."

"I've been authorized to call on you, though."

"Of course, of course. But I live in a state of truce. I am known to be useless, you see."

"You are known to be the greatest expert on European criminal organizations available to me."

"No, no, I cannot enter this affair. There is a tacit agreement. I know so much, yes, that I could be valuable—to them as well as to you. But if I become active, the truce is ended."

"Are you afraid, sir?"

"I do not know."

"You regret living. You could die helping me," Du-

9

rell promised bluntly. "Isn't that what you might prefer?"

The hard mouth twitched. "You call my bluff and ask for my suicide?"

"It may not come to that."

"No, no. I have had my intimation of mortality. I have made a truce with myself, too. It is out of the question. I must refuse you even before you ask."

"But if you could square your personal account?" Durell asked softly.

The blind man lifted his head from the pillow of the chaise and made a small grunting sound. He lifted a shaking hand. "Go away. You disturb me, young man. Your presence here is dangerous to yourself and to me. I am content."

"You're lying. You're not satisfied. You said you wished for death, and now you wish only to be left alone." Durell paused. "You can't have it both ways."

Anger hardened the wide mouth. "You come here and dare to speak to me like this?"

"I'm rather desperate, sir. I need your help. Your knowledge. I'll force it from you if I must."

"You couldn't force anything from me, young man. You forget who I am."

"I know who you *were*, Colonel," Durell said. "And I'm counting on that. I told you I want Kronin. But first I must get some information."

"I do not know this Kronin. I will not help you. Leave me alone."

"But you do know Kronin." Durell drew a deep breath. "Kronin ended your life, but he didn't kill you. He's the same man who threw the acid in your face ten years ago in Vienna. He used the name of Pavel Vanek then. In past years he's killed Tony Gordon, Harry Bell, and Lucy Andrews. All good people. Now he plans to kill me. I'd like to kill him first. For both of us, sir."

He sat back and waited.

Colonel Mignon's mouth was pale. He was quiet for a long time. Then he sighed. He said, "What do you want to know?"

2 • • • • • •

IT BEGAN a week ago in Washington.

The cherry blossoms were in bloom, and the trees made rosy splashes of color, like pink dye thrown into the quiet Reflecting Pool. The air was mild. Durell walked along the path beside the pool with General Dickinson McFee. He had been up all night studying the reports McFee had asked him to memorize. His eyes felt as if someone had thrown grit into them.

McFee, who commanded K Section's field operations, was troubled, although he rarely revealed his emotions. Durell sometimes doubted if the man ever had any. He was small, slight, and neutral, a man of gray, and he carried a Scottish blackthorn walking stick, which Durell knew was a miniature arsenal.

"We work with the Bureau on this," McFee began. "It's partially domestic, and they're jealous of their jurisdiction. Amos Rand has already gone to Switzerland. You can leave tonight. Geneva Central will tell you where to find him there. You know Amos, don't you, Sam?"

"He's all right."

"I understand. But it's necessary to work with him. The FBI is touchy, Cajun, and they wanted to handle it alone. Joint Chiefs insisted on this. I know you're looking forward to leave, but it's been cancelled. I had to pick you because you know one of the men we're looking for. It may help."

"I haven't seen O'Malley since we were boys back in the bayou," Durell said

"But he knows you and remembers you and has some idea you're in the business. He came looking for you."

11

"And the Bureau turned him away," Durell said grimly.

"They couldn't know at the time how much there was to his story," McFee said patiently. "And there are three of them, you know. O'Malley, Bruno Brutelli, and Joey Milan. You saw the dossiers?"

Durell nodded, and they turned onto a path away from the Reflecting Pool. McFee swiped at dandelion heads with his deadly walking stick. It made Durell a bit nervous. And it disturbed him to have a personal element intrude in his work. Emotion tended to blur judgment, slacken reflexes, and cause that split-second pause that could be fatal.

He remembered Frank O'Malley well. A laughing boy who dared anything, back in the bayou days. They had gone to school together, chased girls together, explored and hunted in the swamps as a team. For years they had been inseparable. Then Durell went north to Yale and later to war and he no longer knew O'Malley.

His real name was François, and he was the son of a migrant Texas Irish wildcatter and the Cajun daughter of one of Peche Rouge's leading families. He made an odd mixture of Acadian French and Irish. Last night Durell had seen photos of him from the Bureau's files. He had grown into a lean whip of a man, with gray in his dark straw hair, hollow cheeks, with a wariness in his blue eyes. But the infectious and reckless smile still curved his sensuous mouth, and the mockery still glinted in O'Malley's cat's eyes, even in the dossier's blurred and formal clippings.

"Your friend O'Malley," McFee said abruptly, "is a hoodlum pretending to a sudden access of patriotism."

"He's a gambler," Durell said. "There's a difference. He started young. Opened a gambling ship off Galveston. He's made more money in one night than I'll ever see in my lifetime. He's had enough enemies, but he stayed clean and alive, and the big syndicate people took him in, I understand."

"His two friends—" McFee said distastefully, and paused.

According to the dossiers that had kept Durell awake

12

the night before, Bruno Brutelli was an ex-wrestler who had killed a man in the ring and became a collection enforcer for the syndicate. Joey Milan, a wizened little ex-jockey, was barred from every race track in the country for a long list of violations. The records were unsavory. And yet—

"O'Malley has a good war record," Durell said. "Vietnam for ten months. Special Forces A Team at Ank Dap, working the Cambodian Border in the Highlands, fighting VC and Viet Minh down from Hanoi. Ten months in the jungle, General. He saw what the Congs do to the villagers there. He took some metal in his leg and sat it out in a Japanese hospital for two more months before he returned to Las Vegas and his gambling joint some weeks ago. According to the records, he found everything changed."

McFee slashed at another dandelion head. His eyes were bleak under the pink cherry blossoms. Tourists walked by, swinging their cameras. "You've got to find them, Cajun," said the gray man. "Find them before they kill themselves or get killed."

"Somewhere in Europe?"

"We know O'Malley and his two friends landed in Switzerland. You find out just where. Get to them. Verify O'Malley's story. Get to the upper echelons who've put the mark on those three men. Smash it. And do it quickly." McFee was urgent, anxious.

"It's not a nice job," he added. "Perhaps more distasteful than most. Touchy, because the Bureau properly belongs in it, too. You may have to kill them, Samuel, rather than let Kronin get them. And you must be careful," McFee added mildly, "not to let Kronin get you first."

Six weeks ago there had been an explosion in a vital defense plant that manufactured components for infrared missile detection devices used in the new DF-4 jets allocated to Southeast Asia. It was the only factory in the country that fabricated these parts. The explosion delayed production for three weeks. The FBI investigated quietly, without publicity, and reported it as a case of sabotage.

One week later the water supply of a Midwestern town on the Ohio was found polluted by a contaminant that caused extreme dietary distress among the population. It was quickly corrected. But it could have been worse. The contaminant might easily have been a deadly poison.

Again the classified files of the FBI reported strong suspicion of sabotage.

Top secret blueprints in a NASA office in Houston were found to have been moved and presumed to have been stolen long enough to be photographed before being replaced.

A wildcat strike of a small local union heavily dominated by criminal elements delayed production for five weeks on the new M-14 rifles destined for the Vietnam fighting.

A top biological warfare technician attached to the Colorado research unit vanished for two weeks and was found in a hut in the mountains, brutally tortured and murdered.

There were others.

"It's organized," General McFee said quietly. He waggled his blackthorn at the Washington Monument. "There was something in O'Malley's story when he told the FBI clerk, after asking for you, that he found everything changed in the syndicate he worked for, after he came home from Vietnam. O'Malley may be a thief with a heart of gold—"

"He's a gambler," Durell corrected stubbornly.

"Yes, yes. And a member of the Fratelli della Notte. The Brothers of the Night."

"I never heard of them, sir."

"A euphemism, Samuel, for the same type of outlaw organization as the Mafia, the Cosa Nostra, what-have-you. O'Malley claimed he was on the run, with his two friends, because he refused to go along with new orders that slanted all their operations toward planned sab-

14

otage. He claimed that all the things that had happened to date were simply test forays. To check feasibility and probabilities of success. The network is enormous. It stands poised to cripple every part of the country at any moment deemed desirable by this nation's enemies. It's a knife at our jugular vein. It is dangerous. It is critical. It must be stopped. And you will stop it."

McFee paused. Durell said nothing.

"O'Malley reported," said McFee, "new faces and new people in the Fratelli top ranks. And new orders. Until then, he said, he ran an honest shop at his casino." McFee grimaced slightly. "Bruno Brutelli worked as a strong-arm collector for the numbers operation in Los Angeles. And Joey Milan, the jockey, was back at his old business as a second-story man. He is a human fly, apparently. His orders sent him into many places but not to steal money. He went in for data on power plants, defense factories, missile silos, city water supplies. You name it, Cajun, and you have it."

"Then, why didn't the FBI take O'Malley's information at face value?"

"It came before all the evidence had been collated through their computers. A clerk interviewed him. O'Malley asked for you. He couldn't know about K Section, of course. All he knew was that you worked in some such organization. Of course, when no information was available about you, he walked out. Twenty-four hours later a hold order was broadcast for him. It was too late. He had flown to Europe with his friends."

"I wonder why?" Durell murmured.

"That's for you to find out. They're after him. His outfit, the Fratelli della Notte, considers him a traitor. A defector. He's marked for death. You can save him— or kill him, if necessary, however the truth comes out."

"O'Malley is an old friend," Durell said.

"Can you do it?" McFee asked.

"If I have to."

"Can you find him?"

"I'll find him."

"Do so—before Kronin gets him." McFee waggled his potent walking stick again. There was a small phosphorus bomb in it, tear gas, a dagger, a pistol—all built into the innocent blackthorn. They were anonymous in the throngs of strolling tourists who had arrived in the District for the Cherry Blossom Festival. McFee went on. "The Cosa Nostra, the Mafia, the Fratelli —a rose by any other name, Samuel. I admire your loyalty to old friends, and yet I deplore it. O'Malley's organization is on a sabotage footing—for when, as, and if. And it's being run by Karl Kronin. And now Kronin knows about you." McFee's gray eyes touched Durell's hard face briefly. "You've tangled with Kronin a few times, haven't you?"

"Yes, but not successfully."

"There was a leak in the Bureau somewhere. Otherwise, they wouldn't know that O'Malley went calling on the cops for you. O'Malley doesn't know our business, but Kronin certainly does. How close did he come to you last night?"

"There were two tries in the last two days." Durell felt no warmth in the sunshine as he remembered it. "Not very imaginative. But they'll get better. One was a taxi that apparently blew a tire and ran up on a sidewalk and almost greased me to the wall. Last night was a little touchier. It was a faked Code B message from you. So I left my apartment at one o'clock in the morning. There's a park across from the building, and the gunman was waiting there. Standard silencer equipment. I picked it up afterward, and the lab boys have the weapon now—a Russian PP SH. Luckily for me, he missed the first shot because a car came around the corner and intervened. I never gave him a chance for the second shot."

"But the assassin got away?"

"Clean. The park is big and dark at that hour."

"You must be very careful, Samuel. Kronin will do anything to keep you from contacting O'Malley and getting the rest of his information. You must work fast. If Kronin senses defeat, he may push the button, activate his entire—ah—mob, and do inestimable damage to the nation. Spread panic. Economic chaos. Political disaster. Joint Chiefs and the White House kept me up half the night last night, while you—ah—had your stroll in the park. I'd like you to stay alive, Samuel."

Durell permitted himself a small smile. "Are you worried about me, General?"

"Any man can be replaced. But it takes time. I trust you've studied Kronin's dossier thoroughly. You fly tonight to Europe to find O'Malley."

"I know all about Kronin," Durell said.

He remembered every word of the dossier. He hoped it wouldn't be the last thing he ever remembered.

SUMMARY, K Section File 22 Zeta 5: ── ── ───

Kronin. Karl Antonescue, alias Johan Borg, alias
Pavel Vanek, alias Pierre Dumas, alias Donald Dunn,
alias Kapek Kromsky:

Age: 42

Birth: Believed born Sofia, Bulgaria, 1924, father
a merchant shot by Nazi counterintelligence units
Abwehr 1942, August. Mother d. tuberculosis Soviet
prison camp Novokirsk, Siberia, 1951. No siblings.

Education: Sorbonne, Paris, geology degree, trans-
ferred law and political science. Two years Egypt,
Saudi Arabia, followed by term in Prague. Merchan-
dising enterprises throughout Europe, international
oil trade, finance.

Description: Six feet, four inches, eyes brown,
bald, brachycephalic, wounded by guerillas Greek
Civil War running guns to both sides. Left leg am-
putated above knee. Uses prosthetic aluminum limb
of own design. Slight limp. Above average strength,
intelligence, health. IQ Sorbonne: 159.

Analysis: It is known that subject is an active,
independent agent dealing in military and political
and economic intelligence, selling data to highest
bidders without moral or political scruple. Headquarters a villa near Lugano, Ticino, Switzerland.
Swiss authorities have no evidence to inhibit activity or deport. Subject suspected head of assassin
organization for political effect in Congo, Nigeria,
Southeast Asia, France, Morocco, Poland. Believed
owner of gambling casinos in Riviera, Spain, Italy.

Suspected by U. S. Narcotics Bureau of operating the Green Line of opium smuggling from Red China via Lebanon to South America, possesses strong links with criminal organizations in the U. S.

History: No arrests. No photographs. Operates with known murderer, Anton Dugalef, Albanian member Star-jek Cell Number Six.

Prognosis: Subject is most dangerous. As an independent agent, cannot be trusted for operations of any kind. His organization is believed responsible for the disappearance of three K Section operatives from Geneva Central, London Control, and Naples Central. His known personal appetites for women, money, and luxury are subject to private perversions. He is believed responsible for the disablement and retirement of Colonel A. G. Mignon of Section C2/Theta. (See File Theta 22/6.)

Instructions: K.O.S.*

*Kill On Sight

DURELL put on dark green sunglasses and nodded to the heavy-hipped servant woman who closed the bronze gate of Mignon's villa after him. It was almost noon. He had a rented black Caravelle, parked close to the ornately trimmed shrubbery alongside the black-topped road. He looked to the right and left and up the steep pitch of the wooded mountainside that rose up out of the lake shore. Nothing. No one. The birds sang. A squirrel chattered. The sound of a boat motor echoed up from the glittering surface of the water. It was hot and breathless in the lee of the villa, where the breeze could not reach him. The scruffy palm trees in the garden at his back reached dusty feathers to the Ticino sky.

But something was out of focus.

He had checked in at Geneva Central yesterday, when his jet landed there, and conferred with Arnie Thompson, the K Section resident in the bookshop on the Grande Rue of the old quarter, near the cathedral. Thompson had arranged for the little black car. Its radio, he explained, was two-way; the special frequency would always get someone at the Geneva listening post. Thompson had no information on Kronin's headquarters at Lugano except to say that it was reported deserted and Kronin abroad somewhere. Arnie had wanted him to give up his snub-barreled .38 S&W and use a Walthers instead, but Durell had declined. He preferred the feel of the .38 in its inner holster just under his left armpit. It did not bulge in his dark blue suit.

Something was different.

He could sense the change since he had gone into the

villa an hour ago. The shadows had shifted, the sun was higher, the road curving to the left and into the nearby tunnel high above the lake was in bright sunlight now. The tunnel mouth looked darker.

He did not glance about overtly as he turned to the parked car on the grass verge beside the road. But all his instincts were suddenly honed to a painfully sharp intensity.

He was being watched.

He had left a briefcase on the leather bucket seat under the red plastic wheel. There was nothing important in it. Without touching it, he saw that the case had been moved. Only an inch, but it was enough.

It could have been a child passing by. A potential thief, who found himself disappointed. Perhaps one of Colonel Mignon's servants had been curious.

He didn't think it was any of these things.

Up in the conifers that grew on the mountainside above the highway tunnel something moved. It might have been the wind, causing a shift of shadows. But something glinted briefly where sunlight touched metal. He tried to identify it from the tail of his eye but could not without looking directly at the place and he did not want to give away his awareness just yet.

Except for the briefcase, the car seemed untouched. He got in and put the key in the ignition but did not turn it. He sat for a moment, taking his time, aware of a sudden dryness in his mouth. Then he slid out again and walked around the small car to the rear engine hood. His heart suddenly thumped a little faster than usual.

When he turned the catch and looked in at the compact Renault engine, he saw the bomb.

It was a tidy little package in heavy, dark gray metal, a professional rig, competently wired to the ignition. If he had turned the key, the car and he would have gone sky-high.

He put his right hand forward to disconnect the device, then checked himself again, fingers on the yellow wire. He began to sweat but not from the hot sunlight that struck at the back of his neck. Very carefully he withdrew his thumb and forefinger from the yellow wire.

21

He looked up at the mountainside. A man stood there, watching him overtly now.

Two cars went by in rapid succession, heading for the Italian border. They were followed by a tourist bus for Como and the Villa Carlotta and Bellagio. Their engines echoed hollowly in the tunnel as they rounded the curve that bored into the mountainside.

The birds sang. Music came from the fishing village far below. Everything had acquired a new intensity and meaning for Durell.

When he looked down again at the booby trap on the Caravelle engine, he saw the second bomb, tucked under the generator, with the second set of wires leading from the one he had almost pulled free.

He was expected to find the first bomb. But the wires from the second were black and taped to the coat of road dust and grease along the engine block, almost invisible. If he had disconnected the first, the second packet of plastic explosive would have gone off as he bent directly over it.

A sure thing.

So it had begun, he thought.

Amos Rand, the man assigned to cooperate with him from the FBI, was waiting for him at the little hotel above Paradiso where they had met that morning. Amos would have to wait, Durell decided. He hoped Amos wouldn't push the panic button and call the Embassy at Berne, where he was normally stationed on security watch. Because he would be quite late after his interview with Colonel Mignon, Durell decided.

He straightened, closed the engine cover with elaborate care, and looked at the colonel's villa. He thought he saw one of the peasant servant women move back from a curtain that stirred in one of the tall second-story windows when he turned his head that way. She had been watching, too.

But it didn't have to mean anything.

The man in the woods above the tunnel was quite another matter.

22

Durell walked toward the gate of the villa as if he had forgotten something and were returning to Colonel Mignon for it. The oleanders and the clipped shrubs that flanked the road screened him from the watcher in the woods on the hillside. The man moved again, as if to keep him in line of sight, and this puzzled Durell, because a professional would have been as motionless as stone at this moment. He was big, a dark, bulking shadow in the piney darkness, and it was his wrist watch that had caught the sunshine and given him away with its brief flicker of reflected light.

It was almost two hundred yards to the tunnel mouth and another hundred up the wooded slope to where the watcher stood. Durell moved behind the screen of clipped shrubbery, hugged the high stucco wall of Mignon's villa, and moved fast, spurred now by a dark flame of anger.

The big man stood in the woods like a monolith, not moving at present, ignoring the still, sticky heat that was like a fog among the trees. A single shaft of sunlight slanted over his massive, hunched shoulders and struck the back of his thick neck like the flat of an axe. The mosquitoes had found him and stung his face and hands badly; he'd had no breakfast or lunch, and since he liked to cook and eat, his stomach rumbled with a steady discomfort that for him was the worst agony he could endure. He had long and powerful arms, the face of a Neanderthal, and stubby legs as tough as oak. He stood rooted in the soft loam of the woods above the lake, solid and implacable and without thought except for the job he had come to do. The gun he carried was a U.S. Army Colt .45, and he had two extra clips to go with it.

He didn't like the woods or the country or anything that didn't have the solid, comforting feel of a city sidewalk under his feet. He had an odd, primitive fear of nature and he would gladly have left his post to return to the comfortable house where the others were waiting. But they couldn't wait. And you did what you were told. There was no turning back. They had you in a hammer lock and they'd break your back if you weren't very, very careful.

They. . . .

Only a few minutes to go. Then he could report back. He moved, looking at his watch. It was past noon. His stomach rumbled emptily. He had the strength of two ordinary men and ate enough for four. Being hungry was awful. He dreaded it almost as much as the countryside made him uneasy. He looked at his watch again. He couldn't see anything down on the road. To hell with it. It was time to go.

Beyond Mignon's villa a footpath led down toward the red and yellow roof tiles of the fishing village, making a series of steps down the steep slope to the lake. Along the verge of the road toward the tunnel, a row of clipped evergreens gave Durell an effective shield. He moved quickly, parallel to the highway, reached the cut-stone face of the tunnel mouth and paused. The shoulder of the hill blocked his view of the spot where the man had been standing. He scrambled up, using small shrubs to pull himself above the tunnel and over the road. A few more cars whined by, echoing under him in the heart of the mountainside. He kept climbing, ducked into the shadows of the pines, and approached the spot where the watcher had been.

But the man was gone now.

Durell swore softly and quickened his silent step through the brush. There was a path of sorts here, winding upward through the pine needles. There was not much he could see in the hot shadows of the trees. The footpath cut sharply right and came out on a small level area where he could look back and down to the terrace of Colonel Mignon's villa. The old man wasn't on the chaise any more. Nothing stirred down there. A chipmunk made a flash of striped browns almost underfoot. He paused and listened. There were small thudding sounds on the hillside above him. He followed, moving quickly and in silence.

He came to a place where the big man had tripped over a root and fallen. The imprint of a massive hand was clear in the soft earth under the pines. He took off his sunglasses and shoved them with his left hand into his breast pocket and took out his .38. The sounds of the other man came from the left, away from the path, which had become almost invisible in the loam. He had lost his way and was standing still, confused. Durell climbed higher, above him, still not actually having his quarry in sight, feeling more puzzled by what seemed to be an unusual ineptitude on the other's part. He started down toward him, moving very slowly, watching every footfall.

There was no sunlight here in the deep woods, and the air was still and stifling. At last he saw his man in a small clearing, turning right and left in uncertainty. He was a huge shadow, moving around the clearing like an animal in a cage.

The man turned at the last moment, squinting, and saw Durell coming. Durell made the clearing in a last quick rush and slammed his gun into the other's big belly.

"Drop it," he said.

"Hey, now—"

"Quickly!"

"Look, how did you—?"

The man spoke English; he was obviously an American. His voice was an animal grumble of puzzlement. He was grotesque and beetle-browed, the ugliest man Durell had ever seen. He wore a gaudy sport shirt under a rough linen coat. His belly was enormous but it did not yield to the prodding pressure of the gun. It was like probing into rock. From under the heavy brows the man's small eyes regarded the .38 with disdain.

"Lay off, pal," he rumbled.

He kept his Colt .45 in big bananalike fingers. Then he looked into Durell's eyes and dropped it, grinned, wiped his mouth with the back of his hand. "You're Durell, hey? The guy they call Cajun?"

"You ought to know. You've been watching me long

enough." Durell's anger was dangerous; he tried to control it. "You gimmicked my car."

"Not me. It wasn't me."

"You were looking straight at it. You saw who did it?"

"It was a repair truck. While you were in the pink house. I figured you had engine trouble and sent for them. Two guys in overalls. They wasn't long."

Durell checked himself mentally. The man had a bumbling, if pugnacious, air of truth. "You're Brutelli?"

"Bruno Brutelli, that's me. We read about you in the paper, and O'Malley said we should come around here and look you up, like he didn't make contact back in the States. Put away the popgun, pal. I won't hurt you."

Bruno made a swipe at Durell's .38, like the casual flick of a bear's paw, and the gun went spinning away into the pine needles. Durell ignored it. He didn't want to kill the man. He slammed a fist into the other's big belly and felt the jolt all the way up into his shoulder. The big man grinned. He reached and caught Durell's arm and twisted it in a wrestler's grip, and Durell, for all his strength, was lifted and slammed into the brush. The breath was jolted out of him. Astonished, he scrambled aside, expecting a boot in the ribs. But the huge man just stood there, turning slowly, enjoying himself, grinning.

"O'Malley says you're tough. Like he swears by you. I ain't so sure, so now we'll see."

Durell tried again. He came up with a rush, slammed a shoulder into the giant's thighs, staggered him, and felt a hamlike hand slam down on the back of his neck, like a falling utility pole. He went down, but the other was off-balance and slipped on the pine needles. Durell dived for him. A heavy foot came up into his stomach. He dodged, and the big man rolled away, like a primeval animal struggling for safety.

Durell knew every trick of the business, but nothing worked against this man's enormous strength. The giant almost yanked his left arm from its socket in his rage to prove himself superior. Durell kicked him in the jaw and hurled him back. The other gave a deep, hoarse yell and scrambled about among the slippery pine needles. He had a thick shock of dark red hair. Durell caught him by his thick neck and twisted, while the huge legs kicked and thrashed. A heel caught him in the ribs and broke his grip. Instantly the big man floundered to his feet. Durell hit him with a right, then a left. The other didn't yield an inch. Durell began to think he might have to kill him after all.

His shoe rolled on something, and he saw that it was a branch as thick as his arm. He picked it up and moved toward the giant Brutelli. Brutelli slashed at it, broke it, and hurled the pieces away. His face was savage now. He came on with lowered head, surging through the piney shadows, his meaning plain.

"Cool it, Cajun," someone said.

Durell wasn't sure he heard the words above the long hiss of his own indrawn breath. He kept his eyes warily on the advancing giant.

"Cajun, knock it off. We've been looking for you, and you made it plain where we could find you."

Durell paused. Brutelli had halted, too. He drew a deep breath and picked up his gun and turned about to face O'Malley.

THE FARMHOUSE stood in a small notch among the hills, about ten kilometers from the lake. It was built of stone, with a yellow-tiled roof and outbuildings that consisted of sheds and a small peaked-roof barn. Terraced fields that were silvery green with olive orchards lifted in giant steps up the mountainsides. At the far end of the valley there was a glimpse of Alpine ramparts, still crested with snow, and the train tracks from the Gotthard Tunnel arrowed down the valley beneath the farmhouse.

The fish fins of a yellow Cadillac with German license plates protruded from the leaning sides of one of the farm sheds. The woman who had greeted them had gone to work in one of the orchards.

"It was the best we could find," O'Malley said. "After we got your message in the newspapers, we figured we might as well come down and scout the territory."

"Did you use that yellow Caddy?" Durell asked.

"Sure. Why not?"

"You have a lot to learn. You're not dealing with punks. You're up against the toughest professionals in the world. Kronin's headquarters is only twenty miles from here. Did you hear what your landlady muttered when we came in?" Durell was angry. *"Les américains affreux.* The frightful Americans. It's all over the canton by now about you and Bruno and Milan holing up on this farm."

O'Malley laughed. "We're not worried."

"Well, I am." Durell stared at the tall, straw-haired man for a moment. "Have you got a phone here?"

"Look, let's keep it cool, Sam. Maybe it's like for old

time's sake, but we've got to clear the slate and get down to business before you call the blues."

"There's a bomb in my car," Durell said tightly. "I've got the ignition key, but somebody may fool around with it and get hurt." He thought, *And if Colonel Mignon hears my car hit the sky right after my visit, it won't encourage him to help.*

The three men looked at each other. Bruno shrugged. Joey Milan bit his fingernails. O'Malley laughed again. "A bomb in your heap? It wasn't us, Sam."

"Maybe not. Then it was Kronin, and if he knows I'm here, he's looking for you."

"No sweat. We can handle it now."

"I want the telephone," Durell said.

"We talk business first. The Feds are here, aren't they? I can guess. Maybe that Amos Rand. That son of a bitch from the Bureau. To him I'm just a crook."

Durell said, "You're making a mistake, Frank. I don't like booby traps. I don't like bystanders getting hurt. And we have no deal yet."

There was a smell like an animal den in the farm house parlor, with its overstuffed furniture and religious pictures and dark crucifix on the wall, its polished plank floor and carved woodwork. Through a doorway he could see the huge Brutelli in the kitchen, stirring a wooden spoon in an iron pot that boiled on the stove. Two guns in holsters hung from an old-fashioned peg rack in the hall, and a Remington leaned near the door.

Seeing O'Malley was like seeing a ghost out of the dim past, Durell thought, from a time when the world was young and filled with wonder. O'Malley hadn't changed much. He had the same hollow face, the thick straw hair, the reckless, challenging brown eyes, the rangy nervousness of a wire-taut body. He wore an expensive silk sport shirt, soft slacks, and English loafers. There was no doubt that he was the leader of the other two and that they gave him complete obedience.

"First we'll eat," O'Malley said easily. "Bruno is fussy about his pasta. If he'd kept his mind on the wrestling mat instead of his belly, he'd have been champ.

You're having fettucini with white truffles. He's a genius and he likes people to appreciate his talent."

"The telephone," Durell said bluntly.

"Bruno says eat, we eat. Just to show there are no hard feelings."

Of the three, Joey Milan, the ex-jockey, was the most nervous. He played solitaire on an ornate pie-crust table near the front window of the farmhouse, where he could watch the road. He was small and agile, with quick, darting eyes in a narrow, pointed face. He spoke thinly.

"I don't like it, Frank. He won't play ball. You been dreaming about a guy you once knew in the bayous, but I can smell a cop and I don't have to run four furlongs to know who's behind me. It's a mistake."

"Two gets you nine he makes a deal," O'Malley said easily.

"You talked Bruno and me into this," Joey whined. "We was satisfied. But no, you had to wave the flag and break away from the field. What's it got us? This crummy shack is the last place we'll ever see."

"The Cajun will help us."

The jockey spat on the polished floor. "He's a cop, and no cop never helped me."

O'Malley smiled at Durell. "Are you a cop now, Cajun?"

"Not exactly."

"I heard you work for the government."

"In a way."

"I tried to contact you in Washington. I went to the Feds. That Amos Rand—he was there then. Like he was bucking for promotion. Me, I still hurt from the lead souvenirs I got in Vietnam. Treated me like I was scum. Started digging out charges on income taxes. Taxes! And a lot of old counts. I saw the pen staring me in the face just because I wanted to do something right for a change. So it frosted, and we ran for it. But you heard, huh, and you came after us, right?"

Joey Milan coughed. "Frank says like you're a spy. He says our business is your business."

"What are you running from?" Durell asked.

30

"The Fratelli della Notte," O'Malley said. He spoke easily, but Milan's face twitched, and in the kitchen Bruno Brutelli grunted as if the words were like a blow in the stomach. Briefly there was fear in the eyes of all three men.

Durell had to use that fear. Twenty minutes had passed since he drove from the tunnel road at Colonel Mignon's villa, and another ten was wasted already here in the farmhouse. It was too much time to lose. He turned and walked into the dark hallway of the house, looking for the telephone. It was in the room across from the old-fashioned peasant parlor in a place of honor on a long walnut table that could have graced any Madison Avenue antique dealer's window. He picked up the phone, and O'Malley's hand banged down on top of his.

"No, Sam."

O'Malley's pale brown eyes had changed. They were no longer glowing or amused. They looked ferocious. Milan and Brutelli each had a gun in hand.

"I'm worried about that bomb in my car," Durell said.

"We didn't put it there."

"All the more reason to worry."

Durell twisted the telephone from O'Malley's grip and began to dial. The other man backed away a step. Milan made a thin sighing sound. Durell dialed Colonel Mignon's number.

"Who are you calling?" O'Malley whispered.

"A friend. Where I left the car."

"Is he in your line of work?"

"He's retired. An old man. Blind. He can help us if he wants to. He promised he would. But if my car gets splashed into his house, he may change his mind."

"All right. So long as it isn't the Feds. I won't deal with them. Not after the shafting I got from Rand."

The cold light faded from O'Malley's eyes. Mignon's telephone began to ring. Durell knew he was in great danger. O'Malley lived in a shadow world that paralleled his own, a world of quick and amoral decisions. He couldn't count on boyhood friendship to keep the man's trigger finger loose. But he had to establish command at once, right now.

"Be careful," O'Malley said.

Durell nodded and listened to the phone ring, far away in Mignon's villa.

It rang and rang. There was no answer. Inside the farmhouse everyone was silent. After the tenth ring he hung up.

O'Malley's face was pale, the skin stretched tightly over his cheekbones. "So forget it, Sam."

"You don't forget a live bomb. I'll have to call Rand." Durell saw O'Malley's eyes grow cold again. "I have to work with him."

"You're pushing me, Sam. I told you, I've got a thing about the Bureau. I'm willing to make a deal with you, but not with that arrogant bastard—"

"The deal is still with me," Durell said. "My word on it. You'll have to take it. And I haven't even begun to push."

He began to dial again. The three men watched him. For a moment Durell wasn't sure of O'Malley. The man was as suspicious as a cornered jungle cat. Perhaps O'Malley had a right to be, he thought, considering Amos' pompous manners.

He and Amos Rand had checked into a hotel late last night in Paradiso, with a view of Monte San Salvatore looming behind them. The lights of the funicular made a string of bright beads against the starry sky. Amos was recently divorced and given to a wandering eye. He had spent a term of service once for the Bureau as liaison man in the Berne Embassy, handling internal security, and because of his foreign service and acquaintance with O'Malley's search for Durell, Rand had been assigned to cooperate, although their relationship was ambiguous because of the Bureau's determination to assert its command. Amos was chunky and outwardly amiable, and looked upon the European trip more as a jaunt to renew old acquaintances with the diplomatic secretarial corps than as a job that might entail danger and sudden death.

The telephone in the Paradiso hotel rang five times.

O'Malley bit his lip. Durell felt his nerves string tight as it rang once more—and then it was answered. A girl's light voice giggled in his ear and said, "Hello? Who is it, lover?"

The words were a slow Southern drawl, thick and sultry. Durell looked across the room at O'Malley, who was scowling. He spoke with care. "I want to talk to Amos Rand."

Another giggle. "He's taking a shower. Are you his partner?"

"This is Durell. Get him out of there. And what are you doing in that room?"

"Why, this is Ginny, Sam. Don't you-all remember me? Ginny Jackson. From the Economic Mission." She gave an exaggerated sigh. "Amos phoned and just asked me to come down, the darling."

"Just like that?"

"You don't have to act so mad about it, Sam."

"Get me Amos."

She giggled again. "A pleasure, suh."

Durell pinched his nostrils, waiting, wished for a cigarette, remembered he had quit smoking, regretted it, and thought of Ginny-with-the-bleached-yellow-hair. She was the niece of a Washington congressman, given a sinecure post at Geneva to get her out of an embarrassing escapade last year. A sexpot with a figure that vibrated provocatively with every move she made. He recalled vaguely that Ginny Jackson had been one of the reasons for Amos Rand's divorce. She was a brainless, lush piece of femininity, and somehow he knew she was standing there stark naked, pink and white, perhaps dripping from the same shower Amos was enjoying—

"Sam?"

"Amos, what do you think you're doing?"

"Take it easy, Cajun."

"Get Ginny out of that place."

"It's all right. Ginny's okay." Amos' voice was slightly slurred, and Durell wondered how much he had been drinking with the girl. "How did you make out with Colonel Mignon?"

"How much did you tell that brainless chippy?" Durell asked tightly.

"Look, I just gave her a ring and told her I was back in the country, and so she came down, is all."

"You gave her the name of our hotel?"

"Well, she asked me—we're old friends—"

"You're a fool," Durell said.

"Now, just because I was relaxing a bit—" Amos had just enough liquor in him to be pugnacious. "Leave my private life out of it, huh? Tell me about Mignon."

"The colonel's promised to get information on the outfit we're checking. By tonight. But something else came up." Durell saw O'Malley stir and lift his gun slightly and he didn't know if O'Malley was warning him to be careful or not. His irritation at Amos could blur his judgment, he decided, and he checked himself, speaking quickly, to describe the bomb in the Caravelle parked outside Mignon's villa. He asked Amos to get to work to defuse it at once.

"Who set it?" Rand asked. His voice was a bit more sober when Durell finished.

"Persons unknown. Kronin has a hatchet man named Dugalef, whose specialty is booby traps. A pro assassin. You read his dossier, didn't you?"

"Yeah."

Durell heard Ginny Jackson complaining in the background. He went on. "If you can help it, don't disturb the colonel. Just defuse the car. He won't have the data he promised until evening. And send Ginny back to Geneva."

"What did the old man promise you?"

"Names and data on the top echelon people in the outfit we're after. If anybody knows, Mignon can get it. Do you want me to spell it out for broadcast?"

"All right, all right. I'll get after your car pronto, boss. Don't get sore."

Durell decided not to tell Rand about finding O'Malley. "Don't get careless," he said, and hung up.

O'MALLEY said bitterly, "That Rand. He didn't believe me, gave me the brush, treated me like a criminal. And I'm just back from playing jungle games with the Vietcong. It's no deal, with him in it. I'm pulling out."

"And where will you go?"

"Plenty of places."

"Is any place in the world safe from the Fratelli della Notte? The way it's being run now?"

"I'll find a spot."

"They'll kill you," Durell warned. "All three of you. They can't afford to let you live. You know too much. You haven't given me a thing yet, but they'll pay any price for you. You can't hide forever."

It was two hours later. The sun had gone down behind the mountains of the Ticino, and long shafts of sullen light poured through the silent valleys of the lake country. There was a sultry feeling to the air, a breathless heat, as if they were about to have an early season thunderstorm.

Amos Rand hadn't called back.

Durell had so far gathered only the primary outline of O'Malley's story. O'Malley was reluctant to commit himself.

The trio had run for their lives. In the beginning, from Nevada, they had tried to go west to the Coast; but the desert road was blocked. The airports were watched; the railroads, covered. They turned east and drove to St. Louis. The hunters were only an hour behind them.

"I spoke too freely," O'Malley admitted. "I asked

too many questions about what was going on. I had a chip on my shoulder, coming back from Vietnam. I smelled something pretty rotten in the outfit. Up to then the syndicate did its usual business. But everything was changed. So I guess I asked too many questions, and they decided they couldn't trust me any more."

O'Malley was a clever man. He lived in the world as if it were a jungle, and his agility saved them twice when their pursuers closed in. Bruno, big and dumb and strong, had an unshaken loyalty toward O'Malley. Joey Milan was more fearful; but he had talents O'Malley needed and he could be bullied and browbeaten along the way.

"Like we're dead men," Joey had whined.

They were three shadows in flight, and each man knew his own transiency. Every door was closed to them. Old friends did not recognize them. They needed help, and there was no help anywhere.

"Where can we go?" Joey had asked.

"Outa the country," Bruno had suggested.

"Like Mexico," Joey had said. "I could ride there. Get a license. Fix a race. We could invest the loot—"

"We stay right here in the U.S.A.," O'Malley had decided.

Joey had been incensed. "What's the matter, you got the patriot bug or something?"

"Yes, I'm patriotic," O'Malley had said.

They had rented a trailer and gone south along the Mississippi into Arkansas. They had been followed. O'Malley had not seen the hunters, but he had known they were near in the night, their cries silent but none the less deadly for the silence. Near Little Rock Bruno had bought groceries. Bruno had loved to cook. Joey Milan had gone shopping with him. O'Malley had found a public phone booth and tried to call an old friend. He had almost run out of friends, but he had had to try.

They had been lucky because they had been all out of the trailer when someone had blown it into a smoking, tangled mass of aluminum and steel.

O'Malley had tried to double back north, but they had been waiting in two cars on the only available road. They had abandoned their rented Chevy and had taken to the woods. They had spent a week in an Ozark hillbilly's shack. They had been hungry and thirsty and tired. It had been cold and raining. O'Malley had made them stay.

"Nothing but canned beans," Bruno had complained.

"Not even a deck of cards," Milan had said.

"You're alive, aren't you?" O'Malley had asked.

When he had thought it safe, he had bought a battered Ford pickup from the mountaineer and gone east again to the river. They had been waiting at the first bridge, the same black cars. They had been chivvied south again, toward Louisiana.

It had been spring, and the river had been in flood. The confusion of refugees running from the lowlands had been a help. It also had trapped them like a noose around their necks, blocking the roads they had wanted to take. But O'Malley had used the confusion to lose themselves. The swollen river had cut rail and road traffic. They had lined up for coffee and doughnuts at a Red Cross canteen, standing in the rain and mud with a hundred other flood victims. At the head of the line one of the hunters had waited.

O'Malley had killed him quietly with a knife he had used in the Vietnam jungles. He had propped the dead man behind the Red Cross shack and had known that time had run out.

"We go into the bayous," he had said.

"That's like nowhere," Milan had objected. "They'll kill us there!"

"They'll kill us anywhere. Besides, I've got a friend in the delta country."

"We've got no friends, you said."

"I'm talking about the Cajun. A man named Sam Durell." O'Malley had been weary. "He'll help. He came from Bayou Peche Rouge and he's our last chance. He'll take a piece of the action." O'Malley had looked ugly. "*Someone* must listen to us!"

But Durell hadn't been in the delta. Still, they had been lucky. The hunters had not been infallible, after all. They had lost the scent in the swamps, which O'Malley had known as a boy, and the trio had chartered a fisherman's private plane to Columbus, South Carolina. From there they had taken a jet to Washington. But at the FBI Building O'Malley had run into the stone wall of Amos Rand's pompous contempt. His story about the Fratelli sabotage organization had been dismissed. They assumed it had been a simple case of hoodlums falling out. They hadn't been able to tell him where to find Durell. O'Malley's resentment had towered into rage; he would not show Rand the list he had stolen from the Las Vegas head office of the Fratelli della Notte. He had finally yielded to Bruno and Joey, and they had fled to Europe, where he had gone through agonies of indecision until he spotted Durell's name in the newspapers and came down into the Ticino to find him.

It grew shadowed in the farmhouse. Joey watched the road from the front window. Bruno cleaned up the kitchen. His pasta had been delicious. O'Malley had flung himself into a chair and sat on the base of his spine, his yellow hair rumpled, his face exhausted. Durell was a tall, dark shadow in the room.

"You said something about a list," Durell said. "Do you have it with you now?"

"It's not complete. It's all I could get. There was a lot more I didn't have time to swipe from the Fratelli." He hesitated, then reached into a pocket and fingered a folded sheet of dog-eared paper. "If it wasn't for you, Sam, I'd burn it up and forget it—after the way Rand treated me. But I guess it's too late for that now, any way. The Fratelli will keep the mark on me for good. I told you, I found everything changed when I got home from Vietnam. The whole organization was geared to something new—defense plants, water supplies, highway bridges, you name it. They're only testing their strength now. A labor strike here, sand in the gears there, water polluted someplace else. And there are new faces in the Fratelli, new bosses, people nobody really knows." O'Malley looked angry with himself. "I guess I went too far to back out now. But Rand makes me wish I'd just shut up. So you take it, Sam. There's a lot more to find out, and that's up to you."

Durell glanced down at the paper. It was a scribbled list of factories, bridges, and city names. Dates had been jotted down after each item, information for future sabotage. He looked at O'Malley and knew the enormity of the man's danger.

One of the dates on the list, jotted after a railroad bridge in Massachusetts, was today.

"I'll keep this," he said. "Have you heard the name of Karl Kronin?"

O'Malley nodded. "What started it all was a girl. My girl. Gabriella Vanini. She's something special. She made me want to come home, you know. She warned me to quit asking questions. If you cross the Fratelli, it's begging to get your throat cut. But I had to look into it. And now I've got to find Gabriella again. She's disappeared somewhere here in Europe. So I came here from Washington."

"Why is the Vanini girl so important?"

"She's important to *me*. She knows the truth about the Fratelli top brass. Related to somebody up there. But she's sort of—uh—innocent about it. I got so sore about what was going on when I got back from Ahk Dap that I told her I had to do something to stop it."

Durell expelled a slow breath. Thunder began to rumble in the long mountain valley. He wished Amos Rand would call back. He wondered what he owed O'Malley. The list, even if incomplete, could be checked out. But these three men were criminals. O'Malley had a charm that always worked him out of the tight spots he'd led Durell into when they were boys. And somehow you always forgave O'Malley for his deceit.

Joey Milan said lugubriously, "It won't work, Frankie. He ain't with us."

"He will be," O'Malley said confidently. But his pale eyes were worried. There was a darkness behind his stare as he regarded Durell. O'Malley got up and went to the front door and opened it and looked down the road that curved into the Ticino valley. His shoulders were hunched, as if for protection against the chill, damp wind that suddenly blew into the room.

"Somebody's coming," he said quietly.

AMOS RAND said, "Now, cut it out, Ginny."

"Oh, lover—"

"I mean it."

But he didn't sound as if he meant it. She had her right hand in his pants pocket as he drove her red Mercedes SL along the lake corniche, and her tight skirt was hiked far up on her thighs. She took his hand and manipulated his fingers inside her leg and sighed.

"There now, lover, isn't that much better?"

The warmth and softness of her made him tremble. He felt like a starving, thirsty man who'd been lost in the desert for many years. And Ginny was a hot little animal, twisting and gyrating, soft and wet and pliant, her small white teeth biting him here and there; her tongue had searched him in the shadows as they tumbled about the big bed in the Paradiso hotel room.

It was going to rain. He was worried because he was late, having ignored Durell's urgency about the bomb in the car, and he hadn't taken care of it yet. But with Ginny in bed beside you—

Ordinarily he was a competent man in his job, and his record was a good one. But he was off-balance these days, since his divorce from Janet—how cold, how still, how martyr-suffering-condemning she was in bed! And finding Ginny like this was a shot in the arm to a dying man. Ginny flattered him, inflated his ego, made him feel like something again. He knew her for what she was—empty-headed, frivolous, oversexed, vain, and greedy as a child. No matter. She served her purpose. The images of her pale, silken body—buttocks and warm

41

globular breasts, eagerly clasping thighs—filled his mind, and he drove erratically for a few moments.

Colonel Mignon's villa was just up ahead. He felt a squirm of apprehension in his belly for a moment and then he saw the little black Caravelle still parked along the hedges beside the road, just where Durell said he'd left it.

So it was all right. He wasn't too late. Nobody had been hurt, and he'd enjoyed Ginny for a couple of more hours—

"Stay in the car," he told her.

Her hand made little squeezing motions in his pocket, and she giggled. "Can you leave me now, lover?"

"It won't be for long."

"I can't wait. Oh, I can't wait!"

"Just a minute, sweetheart."

He felt a bit dizzy when he drew away from her and elbowed the Mercedes door open and stood on the edge of the road. Thunder rumbled in the mountains. The lake was the color of dark slate under the heavy evening sky. Mignon's pink villa had taken on tones of ochre and dark red. No lights shone in the upper windows. Everything was quiet, safe. All to the good.

He took a handkerchief and dried his palms as he approached Durell's car and lifted the engine bonnet. Amos knew all about bombs. He'd taken expert courses in demolition and dismantling every imaginable device. He stared down at the twin charges, the one attached to the wiring, the other under the generator. Simple. No trouble at all. And yet—

He dried his hands again. Ginny tapped the horn of her car, but he didn't look up. Doubt clouded Amos' brown eyes. He had a young face, although he was almost forty and felt as vigorous (Ginny could testify to that) as when he was twenty. He was proud of his taut, compact musculature and his hairy barrel chest, although he was always aware of his short stature, which sometimes made him self-conscious next to tall men like Durell. But Durell was too serious, too dedicated, a strange man you couldn't reach or really talk to or understand. He was hard to work with. You always had the feeling he didn't need or want you, didn't quite trust your competence, and kept inviolate a small, reserved corner of his implacable mind.

Amos Rand drew a deep breath and reached into the engine and touched the yellow wires to the generator bomb. It was shadowed in there. The light was bad. He couldn't see under the glob of plastic attached to the grease and gunk of the generator. He felt about with his fingers, felt the soft warm grease—thought of Ginny—and then held his breath. A cold burst of sweat broke out all over him, from forehead to groin—and he pulled the wire free.

Nothing happened.

He blew out his lips with a little fluttering sound and looked at his hands. They were shaking. But the rest was easy. Quickly, with practiced moves, he worked on the ignition wires, detaching them methodically, loosening the little canister of explosive that was enough to blow him clear over the roofs of the fishing village into the lake below. A few drops of rain fell. Ginny tapped her horn again because the top was down on her car. But he didn't hurry. When he had everything detached and tested and safe, he picked up his little tool kit, pocketed it, took the two bomb devices, and walked toward the Mercedes, studying them.

When he looked up, he saw that Ginny was gone.

"Ginny?" he called.

"I'm here! It's raining!"

She had found a small footpath leading to a summer house just beyond the walls of Mignon's villa. He saw the flick of her skirt and legs as she entered the little rococo structure, and grinned. That Ginny. Never enough. He tossed the two bombs, perfectly safe now, into the back of the Mercedes and followed her, his legs still a bit trembly.

It was dark and shadowed in the gazebo. The little building still held much of the sultry heat of the day just ending. He saw the gleam of her shoulders as she slipped out of her silk blouse. She never wore a bra. Her breasts moved as she swung toward him, and he reached for her eagerly now, glad the job was over, glad he could

43

relax and enjoy living again. Her hips slammed against him, squirming, demanding. They sank down to the straw carpet of the summer-house floor, her teeth nibbling at his ear, his hands sliding over her firm, smooth belly into the wetness and the softness—

"Stand up, please," someone said.

The words, in English, came like a blow in the back of the neck. Ginny checked her wild movements and jerked her hand from his trousers as if she had been stung. Amos turned his head and looked at the thick shadow that blocked the doorway he had just entered.

"Who—what do you think—?"

"You are Amos Rand?" the man asked.

Amos could not see his face. "Yeah. And suppose you just take off—"

"You are Durell's friend? His associate?"

Amos wished the light were better. The man had a bullet head that might have been shaven bald, but he wasn't sure. Ginny made small whimpering sounds of outrage, pretending modesty, but her breasts were bare, and she knew it and she wanted the other man to look at them.

"You are stupid," the man said. He had an accent Amos couldn't identify. The man took out a gun with the narrow cylinder of a silencer on it and pointed it casually at Amos. "Get away from the girl. Be careful. Move slowly."

Ginny said in a high, unnatural voice, "Now, look here, whoever you are, this is none of your business, I think it's just terrible—"

"Shut up," the man said distinctly.

"What—what are you going to do?" Amos asked.

"I want O'Malley's list."

"I don't know what you're talking about. Who are you?"

"You do not have O'Malley's list?"

"No, I never saw it—"

"Well, it makes no difference," the man said. He pointed the gun more closely at Amos. Amos felt stupid, sitting there on the floor, his pants half down around his knees, the smell of Ginny's lipstick and perfume and

44

body in his nostrils. He smelled something else and knew that the smell came from himself, one of mortal fear.

"What are you going to do?" he asked again. He couldn't quite believe what was happening. It was all so fast, so unexpected. "Why the gun? I don't know you. I don't know anything about O'Malley or any list—"

"That is too bad. Where is Durell?"

"I don't know."

"Be very certain. I will ask you again. Where is Durell at this moment?"

Amos spoke with sudden anger. "To hell with you, I don't know—"

The first shot took him right in the middle of his thick, hairy chest, picked him up and skidded him backward on his backside and slammed him against the fragile wall of the summer house, legs up and kicking. Amos looked at him with astonishment. He didn't feel anything.

"But you don't have to—" he whispered. The moment he spoke, the blood came gushing up through his throat from his torn lungs, a thick and viscous stream, like a second tongue, flowing over his hanging lower lip. He began to cough and strangle.

The man fired a second shot that tore half of Amos Rand's face and skull away, and when Amos' body stopped its reflexive twitching, the man looked at Ginny Jackson, looked at her proud breasts and slim waist and her tumbled bleached hair.

He didn't waste a bullet on her.

He turned and walked away.

IT WAS only the old peasant woman who ran the farm and owned the farmhouse.

Durell watched her drive the rickety Citroen truck toward the barn. She parked it near the shed where the yellow Cadillac thrust its fins out into the damp wind that blew down the valley.

"It's all right," said O'Malley.

"I'm not so sure."

The woman got out and trudged stolidly across the barnyard toward them. She had a flat face and the resentful, indrawn eyes of the peasant, the hard mouth and knobby hands of one resigned to the years of sweat and anguish poured into the soil. She spoke in Ticinese Italian to Durell as he stepped out of the house.

"Signore, you are wanted by the colonel. You are to go there at once."

"Who told you?" he replied in Italian. "You were in the olive orchard."

"My neighbor, Maria Luchese, came and told me. At once, signore."

"I did not tell Colonel Mignon where I was."

"The colonel knows everything in these valleys. People tell him all he wants to know. He is blind, but he sees everything." The woman shrugged. "That is all I have to say. You may go or stay, as you wish."

Durell did not want to use the flashy Cadillac. "May I rent your truck?" he asked.

"You have the power to buy or rent all I have," she said stolidly, without resentment.

"Grazie, signora."

She looked at him with a brief flicker of surprise for

46

his courtesy, then trudged away. O'Malley caught his arm in an angry grip.

"Look, I didn't ask to get involved with the U.S. law or with any colonels or anybody. I gave you the list. You'll need more, and Gabriella Vanini might have it. But I'm not so sure about anything now. I'm not afraid for myself, but I don't trust that Rand. He'll shoot off his big mouth and put Gabriella on the spot. I kind of counted on you to help find her, but with the Bureau in it—"

"Wait for me here," Durell said. "And be careful."

"I'm not so sure. I don't like it."

"You don't have to like it. You bought a piece of this action voluntarily. Now you have to stay at the table until the wheel stops spinning."

"I can find Gabriella myself. I don't want her hurt, can't you understand? And I can't trust anybody now. I learned that in Washington."

"Stay here," Durell repeated.

It took over ten minutes to push the farm truck down the valley to the corniche along the lake. Lightning flickered in the Alps, and rain came down, lightly at first and then with heavier intensity. It grew prematurely dark. A wind came that shook the old truck and made it sway on the road. He met no other traffic.

When he came out through the tunnel, the first thing he saw was his own Caravelle still parked by the hedges and then he saw the red Mercedes roadster. He suspected at once that it belonged to Ginny Jackson and he swore softly, with cold anger, at Amos Rand. Both cars were empty. No one was in sight. He parked the truck directly in front of the bronze gates of the villa and got out, touching his pocket where he had put O'Malley's written list of sabotage targets.

The bombs were gone from the Caravelle engine. He walked to the Mercedes and saw them on the back seat. So Rand had been here. Rand was still here. He saw a lipstick on the floor under the wheel. Maybe Ginny was here, too. He turned a dark face with stark eyes

47

toward the villa, walked back to the gate, and pulled on the ornate wrought-iron bell chain.

There was no answer.

He pulled again and tried the gate. It was still barred. He walked around the wall, ducked under the hedges, and came out below the terrace with its Roman antique statues, where he had talked to the blind old man only a few hours ago. The tumbled jigsaw pattern of village roofs below the terrace looked black now in the falling rain. He could not see across the lake through the curtains of mist that blew across the water. Thunder crashed again. He jumped, caught the bottom flagstone of the terrace floor, slipped back, jumped again, got a better grip, and hauled himself up over the marble balustrade behind one of the pale white statues that glistened in the rain. The light was fading fast. He saw the cushioned settees, where he had sat with Mignon, still on the terrace where they had been before, the backs toward him. No one had bothered to lower the striped awning over them.

Mignon had promised to get him a complete rundown on the recent organizational shifts and replacements in the Fratelli della Notte. If any outsider could get that secret information, the blind man had that capacity. He had contacts everywhere. His knowledge was encyclopedic. Durell knew that Mignon could get him more data than O'Malley, as an amateur, could ever learn. Mignon had promised and he would deliver.

Durell walked quietly across the terrace toward the chaise the blind man had sat in. The tall French windows into the villa were open. The wind blew the draperies in great snapping flutters that sounded like popguns. He saw the colonel's big dark glasses on the flagstones. Then he saw the colonel's gnarled hand, knuckles down, resting on the wet stone beside the glasses. Someone had stepped on the lenses, and they glittered in a hundred fragments, like a tiny puddle of dark green in the rain.

"Colonel?" he said softly. He didn't feel the rain on himself, and Mignon no longer felt it, either.

The blind man lay on the chaise almost exactly

as Durell had left him. He had been brutally beaten about the head and body. His jaw had been broken; and his teeth, smashed and they clung in bloody, dark ivory fragments to his lips, like jagged froth. The hand that rested on his lap had been twisted, the wrist broken, the fingers bent back until they looked like shattered twigs, all at odd angles. The old man's eyes were open, and his face turned upward, and the rain fell softly on the grotesque caricature of his battered features. The old scars and damage done by the acid didn't matter now.

He had died hard.

The villa was empty. The servants were gone. Durell went all through it, room by room, sliding like a dark shadow through the rainy darkness. He kept his gun in his hand and he wanted to use it, wanted to expel the anger in him with one great burst of bloody violence. But there was nothing here. The house was deserted.

He returned to the terrace. He was shaking, his anger was too great, and he wanted to check it somehow. Nothing was changed here. The old man was still dead, forever silenced. Everything he had known was gone for all eternity.

The rain slackened. Water gurgled in the leaden gutters of the villa. He started to pocket his gun, knowing he had come back too late, wondering where Amos Rand might be, what had happened, who had done it, a hundred questions flickering all at once through his mind, slowly eroding the heat of his anger, replacing it with something cold, very hard, very bitter.

He heard someone call his name. It was like the broken cry of a wounded bird.

"Sam? Sam?"

He looked over the balustrade of the terrace and saw the summer house, saw movement in there, blonde hair, and knew Ginny was down in there. It was perhaps fifty yards away. The light was growing worse. The birches and pines swayed in the cold wind blowing upward from the lake, making a lacework through which it was difficult to see.

49

He left the terrace the way he had come, dropping lightly down the wall, his knees loose, rolling away from the terrace and down the slope into brush that grew along the rock ledges of the mountainside. Lights gleamed in the village below. One of the ferryboats from Lugano was coming in.

Ginny was crying in a strange, keening manner, a thin sound that touched his spine with a cold finger. He walked along the ledge until he came to the path above the summer-house door and could look down and inside. Ginny knew he was there. She called his name and rocked back and forth, squatting on the carpet, her pale body gleaming in the dim light, more naked than not. He saw that she held Amos Rand's head in her lap, and her eyes were insane and wild, beyond reach or understanding at the moment.

He did not move.

He thought of Colonel Mignon's advice earlier that afternoon. Of all the mistakes a man could make when someone wanted to kill him. And of the mistakes a man could make when he wanted to kill.

Only his eyes moved.

He saw the shape of the summer house, with a little gilded wooden cupid perched atop the conical roof, one chubby arm outstretched, wet with rain. The path divided at the little lattice building, going to the right and the left. Below it was a stone fence, then a sharp drop of at least thirty feet to the next terraced level. The tiles of another roof gleamed in the rain, just visible over the top of the stone wall. Cypress trees bent and swayed in the wind, making a dark wall beyond that. But there was a gate in the wall, and obviously steps went down the drop in the ledge. The angle was bad, however. The trees were behind him, moving and shifting. He looked to the right, and a car suddenly went by on the road above with a shocking blast of wind and whining of tires and thunder of engine that promptly echoed in the tunnel and took a long time to fade away.

Ginny called to him, wept, and whimpered.

To the right, away from him and away from Mignon's villa, there was another row of cypress trees, marking the property line. He could not see through them to the next house. But there was an *allée* from the entrance to the summer house, a thick privet hedge taller than he, and the gleam of statuary at its far end amid more shrubbery. *Like a target gallery*, he thought. *Go to Ginny, answer her cry, see how badly Rand was hurt* —but he knew Rand was dead—*and when you crossed the* allée—

That was it.

Ginny called a third time. She cradled Rand's bloody head to her naked breasts. She was covered with Rand's blood all the way down to her waist.

He called quietly to her. "I'm coming, Ginny. Right now."

He started down the path, deliberately brushing the shrubs to make them crackle and shower down their burden of raindrops. Nothing else stirred. He was five steps from crossing the *allée* to the summer-house door when he suddenly changed direction. He had been walking heavily and steadily. Now he abruptly swung to the right, above the hedges that formed the *alleé*, and with a speed and lightness born of long training, reflexes, and the instinct of a hunter, he slipped through the rhododendrons and oleanders that grew on the mountainside, moved like a shadow, a grim nemesis, as swift as a dark stalking panther.

He had calculated the time when he might have been expected to cross the *allée*. Five more steps and he would have been exposed. It was over fifty feet to the stone property wall. He couldn't make it in time to prevent the first stirring of alarm in the mind of the man who had to be waiting there for him.

But it was time enough.

He came over the wall with his left hand and rigid arm supporting the long swinging leap of his body, just as the dark shadow who crouched behind the statue at the end of the *allée* began to rise. He saw the man's flat face, the Tartar cheekbones, the wide mouth still fixed in a faint, superior smile of anticipation. He saw the gun, the cylinder of the silencer, the way he had been

51

set up for it, just as he had thought, like a target at the end of a shooting gallery.

His .38 would be too noisy. He didn't want to use it. His right hand flashed and caught the man's gun wrist with the edge of his palm. Bones broke with small popping sounds. The man's wide mouth opened like a fish, his eyes bulged, and he made a small sound of dismay, while a look of black rage and despair flickered in the eyes under his shaggy brows. The gun with the silencer skidded into the brush. The man came up with a lunge, his raincoat dark with wet about massive, heavy shoulders. He took Durell in the belly, and Durell fell off-balance, came down off the wall all the way, rolled, came up like a big cat, and chopped at the thick, bulging roll of fat at the nape of the man's neck. The assassin fell forward, tried to check himself with his hands flat on the ground, and collapsed with his broken wrist folding under him. Durell chopped at the neck once more and then aimed a last and careful blow.

There came another cracking of bone, more distinct this time. Blood vessels ruptured. Neural centers were crushed. The man's head fell to one side at an awkward angle. His neck was broken.

Durell dropped to his knees beside him, breathing in long, strained gasps. The rain felt cold on his face when he looked up at the darkening sky.

"HE KILLED Colonel Mignon," Durell said quietly. "He killed Amos Rand for really no good reason at all, except that he liked to kill. Murder was his business. Mignon said Kronin might make the mistake of sending someone else to do the job on me. But Kronin won't make the same mistake again."

"Who was he?" Arnie Thompson asked.

"Among other names, he called himself Mahmud Dugalef. Algerian, Albanian, Swiss citizenship—you name it," Durell said. "Dugalef would have any papers needed, provided by Kronin. He was one of the most expert assassins in the business. He was Kronin's shadow. We spotted him last in the Congo. We've got his dossier at Annapolis Street, and NSA has him filed at Fort George Meade, the French have him in the Sûreté, the British in their M-six records. Probably Moscow has him listed at Number two Dzherzhinsky Square, too. Peiping's L-five Group used him in Hong Kong. He was always linked with Karl Kronin."

"Well, Dugalef is dead now."

"And it's a mess," Durell said.

It was almost dawn of the next day, and he felt a bone-heavy weariness, a grittiness in his eyes from lack of sleep. He had called Thompson in Geneva at once from Mignon's empty villa. He needed help to clean it all up. There was no point in involving the local police and getting stories in the newspapers, starting a wave of international rumors. In Durell's business a cardinal rule was to keep things quiet.

Everything had gone wrong that could possibly have gone wrong. Perhaps if Rand had gotten there sooner, perhaps if he had gone alone instead of succumbing to Ginny's charms—or perhaps if he himself had been more persuasive with O'Malley—

Because O'Malley was gone, too, with his two friends, Bruno Brutelli and Joey Milan.

When he finally got back to the farmhouse, it was only to learn that the three men had cleared out everything, without a trace or hint of their destination. They had taken the Cadillac but only as far as the railroad station in Lugano, where he and Thompson had found it parked about two hours before midnight. Thompson had called the rental agency in Zurich then and made arrangements for it to be driven quietly back there, without questions. But no one could tell them, in the busy railroad station, where the three Americans had gone, or when.

Arnie Thompson, the Chief Resident of Geneva Central, had been quick and efficient when he arrived. He was a pro, and Durell used his talents without wasted motion. There was nothing to be done about Colonel Mignon; they had to let the police find his body sooner or later. But Dugalef had been dropped into the deep water of the lake, and Amos Rand's body went the same route. There was no help for it. They couldn't stop to answer questions for the police or the newspaper reporters.

Ginny Jackson had been another problem. She was numb, paralyzed with hysteria, her eyes red and swollen and blank with shock. They had managed to clean the blood off her, wash her face, get her clothes back on, and quietly hustle her to the car and to a doctor that Thompson knew who could keep his mouth shut—for a price.

Thompson complained about his budget. "I don't know where we can fit this into the expense records. The accountants will raise hell with McFee."

"Put her under 'miscellaneous,' " Durell said.

"And then what?"

"Pay her doctor and hospital expenses. Keep a man with her as long as possible. Threaten her with scandal

54

if she opens her mouth. Tell her she'll be sent home to her congressman uncle at once if she talks."

"She'll talk." Thompson sighed.

"But maybe not too soon to hurt us."

The doctor had taken Ginny in his own car to a shall, private clinic where she would be given a two-week rest under close guard. She would be all right when she was finally released. But nothing would ever be the same for Ginny Jackson again.

Now, with dawn light breaking over La Salève above Geneva, turning Lake Leman to pure silver, Durell stood in the upper rooms above the bookstore on the Grand Rue that was K Section's headquarters for Geneva Central. Thompson was yawning. He was a tall, spare man, almost bald, with a fringe of golden hair above his ears, a slow and easy manner that belied his quick intelligence and devious mind. He was more than competent, and Durell was grateful for his help.

Thompson had quickly encoded the list of sabotage targets Durell had obtained from O'Malley and used the small, powerful radio transmitter in the attic of the old Calvinist house to notify the London relay office and transship the information to Washington and General McFee. The answer came back at four in the morning. The list checked out: places, dates, targets. A railroad bridge in Massachusetts on the New Haven line had mysteriously collapsed twelve hours earlier. Sabotage was suspected, and it was still being investigated.

The radio reply had a Triple-A URGENT/PRIORITY tag. Durell was ordered to get more data. Get to the top man in the Fratelli. Smash the plot and do it at once.

Thompson's heavily hooded blue eyes were sympathetic. "How? Where do you go from here?"

"I need O'Malley again. He bugged out and he knows more than he told me, I think. Two to five, as he'd say, he's hunting for his girl, Gabriella Vanini. She's his weak spot. He's in love with her, and she's connected to the higher-ups in the Fratelli, somehow. Kronin is certain to connect her to him and cut her out. O'Malley wants to protect her but he doesn't quite trust me because I worked with Rand. O'Malley is a volatile, impulsive man. That's how he got into this mess in the first place—out of anger, and outrage at finding domestic sabotage after he fought in Vietnam."

"If that's all he told you about Gabriella Vanini, then it's impossible to find her."

"We must," Durell said. "Find her, find O'Malley. If I don't get to her fast, Kronin will see to it that they're never found again. We don't have all the data we need, Arnie. But O'Malley and the girl could lead us to the top."

"You need some sleep," Thompson said.

Durell shook his head. "We'll do it together."

He called Lem Gray in London and asked him to check every telephone directory in every major city in every country in Western Europe. It was a long and tedious task, with only small odds for success, but the London office had an F-67 Whirlwind computer, the only one available. He also asked Lem to check with FBI documents for their records on O'Malley, Joey Milan, and Brutelli, using SIPP files—Search and Inquire, Photo Plastics records. Lem called back from London in twenty minutes. Durell could hear the whir and click of the computer working in the background.

"They're feeling pretty shook back there, Sam. They don't like the report on Amos Rand."

"Did you get anything?"

"They got stuffy. They say it's all classified."

"All right. Get me Don Hine at Annapolis Street."

Hine was put to work checking stateside police blotters for data on O'Malley, beginning with Las Vegas, with emphasis on O'Malley's girl friends. By this time it was clear daylight in Geneva, and Durell suddenly realized he had eaten nothing since noon of the day before. His eyes were scratchy as he turned to the little kitchen in Thompson's apartment and scrambled himself eggs and made a pot of coffee and swallowed a tumbler of Thompson's best bourbon. He thought of the massive Brutelli's passion for cookery. Maybe there was something in that; but he couldn't think what it might be.

Lem Gray, using the overseas cable, checked a Major Keenan in the Pentagon for a rundown on O'Malley's military record. "It's better than clean, Sam. Wounded twice, awarded a Bronze Star, was a perfect liaison man with the Montagnards and Viets. They were proud of him. They wish they'd had more like O'Malley with Special Forces."

"What about his payroll records? Any commitments back home?"

"Nothing, Sam. No wife, mother, family."

"Any letters to girl friends, out of censor's office?"

"I asked. They don't keep track of stuff like that."

"All right. Check back with Don Hine, right?"

The search of police blotters in the States showed no local records anywhere. Joey Milan had a count of three burglary charges, a one-year term in Idaho for breaking and entering, and disbarment from the Jockey's Association for complicity in rigging a race at Aqueduct. Bruno Brutelli had done a two-year stretch in Sing Sing for manslaughter. The comments of the police chiefs were invariably bitter.

"They're three of a kind, Cajun."

"Is the name of Gabriella Vanini associated with them anywhere?"

"Sorry. Nothing, Sam."

"Let Don Hine give it up, then," Durell said.

Lem Gray was dry. "He has, old buddy, he has."

The computers in London reported hundreds of Vaninis in the telephone directories, from Hamburg, Germany, to Catania in Sicily. So far there was nothing on a Gabriella Vanini specifically. Durell paced Thompson's little apartment. The hours went by. He knew he was pushing himself beyond the edge of reasonable fatigue. He brewed more coffee and finished the bourbon. Then he got out maps of Europe and began checking bus, railroad, and airline schedules out of Lugano. But it was only a short jump from the lakes to Milan, in Italy, and it was like counting the holes in an enormous seive from there. O'Malley could be anywhere by now.

Noon came and went.

Lem Gray called back from London. "It's hopeless, Cajun. The machine has given up."

"All right, Lem. Thanks, anyway."

At three in the afternoon Durell sat bolt upright out of a sound sleep. He had dozed in a chair beside the telephone. Thompson was downstairs in the shop. Traffic sounds came up from the narrow street below. Durell considered the thought that had wakened him for perhaps thirty seconds; then he made what he knew must be his last call and his last chance. If he failed, he would fall too far behind in the chase ever to catch up with O'Malley again.

Onan McElroy was the K Section resident in Naples Central. He was a little elfin man who had once worked with Colonel Mignon and knew more than most about Italian secret societies. The telephone rang four times before McElroy's light voice answered in Italian. Durell identified himself briefly in code.

"For hell's sake," McElroy complained. " 'Tis the leprechaun out of the bayous, himself."

"Onan, it's important. You've got to do it."

"Do what, Cajun?"

Durell explained about Gabriella Vanini. "She's just a name. She had to be in the States for O'Malley to have met her, because this is O'Malley's first trip to Europe, so he didn't get to know her here. She's back in Europe now, because O'Malley is looking for her in this area. Maybe she's in Italy, maybe not. But if she was in the States, there's a chance she was traveling on business or work or something and not just a tourist, right? Can you check with Work Permit Records, Emigré Labor Certificates, that sort of thing? The Italian government licenses laborers to go abroad. The girl isn't a laborer, of course, but there might be something like that in the records."

"Cajun, it's siesta time down here. Everything is closed. Maybe in a couple of hours—"

"I need the data now. You can do it, Onan."

There was a long sigh, a yawn, a little grunt. "All

right, will do. My taxi business will suffer, though."

"Hurry it up," Durell said.

An hour later he had it.

"We have the record of the whole family," McElroy said tersely. "The Vanini Family Circus."

"The what?"

"A *circus*. A troupe of traveling acrobats. They claim to have been in the business for over a century. Performed for all the crowned heads of Europe and so forth. Come from Palermo. Everything in the files is clean."

"Is a Gabriella Vanini registered with them?"

"Sure. A trapeze artist. Does a high wire act, a horseback riding act—you name it, the gal does it. The troupe just got back from a three-month tour of the States."

"Good," said Durell. "Where are they now?"

"France, somewhere. They registered the schedule with their agent's office. Hold the line, Sam . . . Here it is. French Riviera. Cagne, yesterday. And a couple of other little towns farther down toward Nice."

"Thanks, Onan. Thanks for everything."

"You owe me something," McElroy said bitterly.

"What's that?"

"An afternoon's siesta."

A LIGHT wind blew over the Côte d'Azur and smelled of the sea and pine woods and fish. The sky was filled with tumbling cumulus that sent long patches of shadow prowling over the fishing boats and the mountainous coast eastward toward the Italian border.

Durell had driven down from Switzerland in the Caravelle. He drove carefully, seeking anonymity in the thick traffic that crawled down from the Alps. The Vanini Family Circus had advertised itself with bright posters splashed along the highway from Cagne to Nice, and he simply followed the signs. He found the circus set up in an empty lot along the stone quai of a half-moon harbor, where bright Riviera yachts were berthed.

He parked nearby and got out. No one paid any attention to him. He looked tall in his dark blue suit, white button-down shirt, and dark knitted tie. The circus was a typical small-town operation, with two aged tents serviced by battered house trailers that had been altered to serve as ticket booths and dressing rooms for the performers. The signs in French boasted a century-old continuity for the "Flying Vaninis, Performers to the CROWNED HEADS OF EUROPE SINCE 1866." The posters were garish and had been used too long. Everything pointed to slow decay and economic failure of the enterprise.

There was a large billboard that advertised: GABRIELLA, THE FLYING BALLERINA. He doubted that the slim, silver-spangled girl with the long hair crowned with a diadem, shown flying between two trapeze bars and hanging by her teeth from a leather strap, resembled

60

the real thing. The cool wind was filled with the sound of mauls pounding stakes, the neighing of a circus horse, the cough of a mangy, caged lion. Clothing hung from the trailers and snapped in the breeze.

"You like her?" Someone spoke in Italian-accented French behind him. "You come see tonight, eh? An artist, she is, our Gabriella. *Molte belle, signore.* She is my aunt."

Durell turned to view a flash of white teeth gleaming under a bristly black moustache. The man was stocky, Sicilian, wearing a gaudy sport shirt and khaki trousers stained stiff with paint. There was pride and love in the fierce eyes that regarded Gabriella's poster.

"Your *aunt?*"

The man grinned. "We have a very complicated family, signore. I am old enough to be her papa, I assure you."

"From your advertisements it looks like she's your whole circus."

"No, no, signore. But she could be. She is a marvel, an angel, the way she flies. She is the bright spirit that gives us all our hope and courage."

"I'd like to meet her," Durell suggested bluntly.

"Pardon, this is not permitted. You are a patron, she is the performer. In our family we do not encourage—"

Durell took out a wad of 100-franc notes and nodded to the big tent. "I won't be in town this evening. Couldn't I just watch her work out?"

The "nephew" eyed the money hungrily and brushed his fierce moustache. He looked sad. "I am sorry." Then he brightened. "Unless, perhaps, you are—what do you call it?—a talent scout?"

Durell took the cue. "I understand a rival firm has been considering Gabriella for a cinema role."

The man's mouth opened. "I hear nothing of this, signore. It is impossible." He shook his round head. "In any case Gabriella would never leave the family. Never!"

"No one else has inquired about her?"

There was a second's pause that told Durell what he

wanted to know. "No one like you, signore."

"But someone *has* been here?"

"An old friend, only." The man scowled. "A trouble-maker who disturbs our angel's heart and drives her to the wind and the sea."

"I don't understand."

"She is not here now. She is out there somewhere." He waved a thick arm at the blue Mediterranean. "She loves the sailboats and goes alone when she can. She will return only in time for performance tonight."

"You have no idea which way——?"

"None. And I think you lie and are bad man, not a talent scout. You are one of them who brings trouble to us. Perhaps police. I do not know. Today one cannot tell blacks from whites."

Durell caught at a splinter of the man's thought. "One of whom? Who do you mean?"

The man assured himself they were out of earshot of the laborers working around the tents. "Signore, I beg of you. If you are one of the Fratelli, leave us alone. We are not involved in your affairs. We interfere with nothing." Fear glinted in his dark eyes. "We ask only to live in peace, eh? We wish to know nothing. Has not Gabriella made this clear? Vecchio Zio has given her a promise of protection——"

"What has she done?"

"Nothing!" The man almost shouted the word. "Is it her fault to be born a princess of the dark, this lovely angel who seeks only sunlight and the wind?"

"Who else has been here?" Durell asked again.

"The Devil himself." The man crossed himself and turned away. "Now I have my work to do."

It could be Karl Kronin, Durell thought, as he surveyed the organized confusion around the circus tents. It all looked innocent. A fisherman's diesel engine knocked at the wind. Traffic droned on the Lower Corniche road. Early tourists in bikinis walked by. All at once he smelled and tasted the danger here and he stared closely at the poster of Gabriella Vanini, with her slim, lovely figure and her dark flying hair. How close was she to O'Malley? Was it significant that she had gone sailing today? She had been disturbed. By O'Malley? Had she gone to find him?

He scanned the blue sea under the tumbling white clouds. Several sails bent out there under the loom of the mountainous coast. They must be early-bird yachtsmen trying their wings on this windy spring day. The needle in the haystack again. He felt frustrated. He had to reach O'Malley and the girl could take him to O'Malley. But Karl Kronin was somewhere nearby. He could feel it in his bones. And where Kronin walked, death walked on his heels.

He went out on the stone quai, where charter boats were moored. Ten minutes later he was aboard a sleek motor cruiser, passing the mole. The captain was a slim teen-ager from Provence in a singlet, duck pants, and sneakers. The varnished plaque over the sky deck announced his name as Jean Dufours.

"Mademoiselle took the *Manta*," he told Durell in English. "A real chick, eh, monsieur? You like my English? It is good, *non*? I learn from American college girls."

"It's good. Can you spot the *Manta*, Jean?"

"When I see it, dad. She went toward Juan-les-Pins. I watch her trying to—how you say it?—cool it. She burns a blue flame."

Durell smiled and began to feel his years. "A bonus for you if we find her in the next half hour."

"You wantto catch her bad?" The boy grinned, showing white teeth. "Another is anxious to catch her, a gentleman your age, and three, maybe four men—damned Germans I think. They took Papa Simone's boat."

"What did he look like—this other man and his friends?"

Jean laughed. "*Voyons*. Bald, dressed for the city, like you. Walked with a limp. Hard yellow eyes. I would not let him have my boat at any price."

He had described, briefly, Karl Kronin. . . .

Durell scanned the mountainous Riviera coast with

63

care. Eastward the resort hotels nestled in their coves and harbors with glittering opulence. To the west, sunlight reflected on a trailer camp located on a small rocky promontory. There was scrub brush, pines, a dark, coarse sand beach, then an area of private villas hugging the steep coast. Jean abruptly throttled his engines.

"Voilà. The *Manta,* monsieur. Below Madame Kronsky's house. The yellow one. She has not yet come down for the season."

"You're sure it's the right boat?"

"I know it well. No one is aboard, though."

The sailboat they sought had been beached on the crescent sands of a tiny inlet under the yellow villa. The trailer camp was a mile to the left, the aluminum trailers and brightly colored tents half-hidden in the pines.

"Take us in," Durell ordered.

They eased gently into the rock-bound little cove. No other boats were in sight. The boy kicked their stern about with a flat ripple of exhaust, which echoed back from the steep slopes. They grounded twenty feet from the red sloop. "She is not here, dad," Jean said.

"We'll go ashore and find her."

"You wish me to accompany you? I thought you wanted to be alone with her, monsieur. A rendezvous—"

"She's in trouble. Have you a weapon aboard?"

The young French boy's eyes gleamed an electric blue. "I have a Remington—pump gun, is it? I use it for the target shoot. I was right, then. I think you are an *agent*—a cop, *hein?"*

"I'm not a cop," Durell said shortly.

"Then it is five hundred extra for me and the gun ashore. In advance."

Durell paid him. "All right."

He waded through the cold water and walked across the dark coarse sand to the red sloop. There was no sign of Gabriella. But a clear set of small footprints led across the beach and a deserted terrace under the closed villa. Jean followed, his rifle held easily in the crook of his elbow. He looked tough and competent.

Durell was sure that Gabriella had come here for a

specific purpose. But her prints led away from the trailer camp to the left. If she had sailed here for a meeting with O'Malley, she'd have headed for the camp. On the other hand, if it was Kronin who had hired the other boat to follow her, then he was desperately far behind. She might have been cut off from her goal. Still, he saw no sign of another charter boat, and when he asked Jean, the blond boy shook his head.

"Papa Simone's boat is not here."

"It should be."

There were only the girl's prints, and this was briefly reassuring. Gabriella had walked close to the water's edge and then clambered over mossy rocks into the woods. Her path then became more difficult to follow. Sunlight dappled the soft turf like gold coins. She wore sneakers, however, and here and there a tread was visible. Durell quickened his stride. Beside the graveled road that led to the shuttered villa she had halted uncertainly, taking a few steps in several directions. Then her prints changed abruptly as she began to run along the gravel, the toe marks deeper. Something had frightened her away, driving her up the mountainside.

"Hurry," he told the boy.

A few moments later they came across several sets of prints in the raked gravel, made by running men. They cut across the steep promontory and turned to follow Gabriella Vanini's trail.

"Two men," Jean said. "Will they be armed?"

"Yes. So be careful."

"What has the girl done, eh?"

Durell's reply was cut off by a thin, faint scream from the woods above. It could have been the lonely cry of a bird, but he knew it wasn't. It came from beyond the private driveway that looped down to the yellow villa. He ran faster. The boy kept pace with an easy, loping stride.

"Papa Simone's boat," he called softly.

In another cove, invisible from where they had landed, was a moored motor cruiser. Durell spared it a quick glance from their height above it but did not slacken his pace. He thought he saw someone still aboard, glimpsed

65

through the intervening pines. A bald head, a very tall and menacing figure, even at this distance. Kronin? But it was too far away to be certain.

The girl screamed again.

Then they heard the heavy, booming shot.

As if it were a signal, scores of seabirds lifted from the rocky, wooded slope and flew screeching into the blue sky. Their cries wiped out any immediate reply to the shot. Durell plunged upward through the shadowed pines, his feet slipping in the needles. He dropped flat behind a thin, gray shelf of granite. The young skipper kept up with him.

"There they are," Jean breathed.

There were two of them, squat and somehow alien to this quiet place, wearing heavy city clothes. One, with a gun in his hand, walked balancing on a spine of rock toward a copse of trees near the crest of the promontory. Beyond him sea and sky shown benignly. The Riviera coast was hazed by distance toward the Italian frontier. The man wore a narrow-brimmed gray hat and a dark topcoat with a velour collar. The second man was circling right, through the woods. The girl was not in sight.

Durell drew a tight breath. Jean lifted his rifle. "I could give them both a *piqûre* of lead, eh?"

"Wait."

"But they hunt her like she was a wounded bird."

"Let's spot her first," Durell said.

There might be more men from the other boat, circling the mountainside to cut off Gabriella's flight. He couldn't chance surprise. Defeat could mean a bullet in the back of the head. But why the girl? She hadn't been mixed up in the business in Switzerland. Was it all just a blood feud for breaking the tribal rules of the Fratelli della Notte? In any case it surely meant that O'Malley was nearby, and she had come to meet him in this lonely place.

But why was Gabriella Vanini, an acrobat in a two-bit gypsy circus, so important? He had to keep her alive to answer his questions.

The man in the narrow-brimmed hat still probed along

66

the tiny cliff-edge. The other had crossed the patch of woods and was climbing higher. He came out of the pines and yelled to his companion, and they both broke into a run.

Durell started up—and swore softly as the boy beside him lost patience and fired at the man on the rocks. The sound was enormous and then it was snatched away by the sigh of the sea wind. The man on the ledge staggered and turned a dark, shocked face toward them. Then he fell or dropped beyond the crest of the hill. Durell did not know if he had been hit or not.

"Come on," he snapped.

They had lost the advantage of surprise now. He waved Jean to the right and plunged into the pine shadows. The man there had disappeared. Then he saw a small rustic cabin that cast dark shadows on the woody slope. The girl was hiding there, flattened against the peeled-log back wall. She wore dark slacks and a white blouse under a rumpled sweat shirt that had holes in both elbows. He saw everything with a sudden, sharp clarity that took in the details of her enormous frightened eyes, her wind-tangled hair, her open mouth straining for breath after her flight. She looked like a small animal gone to ground after pursuit by a pack of hunting dogs. . . .

Pine needles spurted at her feet as he heard another shot. A third bullet splintered wood from the hut. She pressed deeper into the shadows. But there was no other place for her to go.

Durell swung right and climbed the steep slope toward the shots. He wondered about the second man Jean had shot at. But he couldn't stop now.

The gray fedora showed briefly through the thick pines. He did not fire at it. The man was thirty yards away, still above him; his attention was focused on the girl. Durell was sure now that they meant to kill her. He climbed faster, his shoes digging into the slippery pine needles. At the last moment the other suddenly whirled, topcoat flapping in the wind, and fired at him. He did not feel the bullet pass his head except as a slight *puff!* that disturbed the sound of the breeze in the trees.

He squeezed the trigger twice. The man lost his hat, threw up an arm, and fell, rolling over and over down the slope. At the same moment he heard a yelp of fear and another shot that was not Jean's weapon. He spun back toward the gravel road in the trees. The boy was sprawled beside it, his rifle lost a few feet from his outstretched arm. His yellow hair looked pale in the sunlight. The second man was scrambling down after his gun.

Durell shot him three times and watched the body tumble bonelessly down the slope toward the little beach far below.

"Jean!" He knelt beside the youth. It was a shoulder wound, and the boy's eyes flickered as Durell gently turned him over. Jean coughed, but there was no blood in his mouth.

He looked blind for a moment, then asked, "Did you—did you give him the *piqure*, dad?"

"They're both dead."

"And the young lady?"

"All right, I think." Durell watched the boy smile. "I must leave you for a moment. I have to get her."

"Je resterai ici." Jean struggled up, holding his shoulder. Then he suddenly gulped, turned white, and fainted from the pain.

Durell stood up and turned back up the slope to the little cabin where the girl had been hiding.

She was gone.

"GABRIELLA!"

The wind mocked him and snatched her name away. He saw her footsteps in the gravel around the cabin, running toward the body of the first man he'd shot. He followed cautiously until her trail was lost in the pines.

"Gabriella!"

He heard the shot; she was a better marksman than the hoodlums who had hunted her. The slug tore a rip in the sleeve of his coat. Quickly he put down his gun and held his hands out, palms upward.

"Gabriella, don't shoot again!"

He could not see her, but he admired her presence of mind. When he went back to Jean, she had run from the cabin and snatched up the dead man's weapon. She thought he was another of those after her. He felt a cold sweat as he walked steadily toward her and called out in English.

"I'm a friend of O'Malley's!"

Her voice was thin but steady. "Stop where you are."

"I only want to talk with you."

"I don't wish to talk to you or anyone. Stay away from me. The next time I shall shoot to kill."

He didn't doubt she could keep her word. But he kept walking. He saw her now, slender and straight, as she stepped from behind a thick pine tree. He walked past the man who had worn the hat. He was quite dead. His face was just a face. He thought of Kronin, down in the cove on his boat, and knew there would be others.

"I warn you ..." the girl called.

He was near enough to see the desperation in her eyes. She breathed shallowly in her loose sweat shirt, but there was a hint of a fine body under the ragged garment, caressed by ripples of the Mediterranean wind. He halted.

"Gabriella, where is O'Malley?"

"Who are you? Why do you want to kill me?"

"I don't. I followed you to help you."

She bit her lip, and he decided he was close enough to risk it now. No time to argue with her fear. He made a quick grab for her gun, but the girl was almost too fast for him. She got it up and fired. The muzzle flame blasted past his ear as he caught her wrist and deflected her arm. The next moment he hooked a heel behind her foot and yanked her aside.

But it was like trying to hold a wildcat in his bare hands. She was strong, in perfect condition, thanks to her acrobatic performances; she was as agile as any trained judo expert. She scrambled away, and he tackled her, and they tumbled down and over each other on the slope. Her nails raked his face. Her thick hair swung wildly, and he felt her firmness and at the same time knew the womanliness of her as he landed on top of her near the bottom of the slope. He let his weight rest on her and pinioned her arms above her head. He was panting.

"Now listen, Gabriella. We have no time left. Do you want to get away or not?"

"Who are you?" There were tears in her eyes. "You can kill me, but I'll never take you to O'Malley!"

"My name is Sam Durell," he said tightly. "And you'll take me to him and Joey Milan and Bruno as soon as we clean up around here."

"O'Malley mentioned you—"

"He came to me, and I turned him down, but now I've changed my mind. We'll talk on the way. Come along."

He pulled her to her feet. She made awkward feminine dabs at the pine needles on her clothes and tried to straighten her tangled hair. He went back and picked up the gun he'd taken from her, then retrieved his own. He threw the hoodlum's gun far out over the steep slope into the sea below. Then he took her hand. "Hurry."

They found young Jean sitting up and holding his shoulder beside the second dead man. The girl looked in despair at the second body. Durell was grateful that the yellow villa nearby was not occupied. There had been no alarm.

"Jean?"

"I—I think I can return to my own boat," the boy said. "Is the young lady all right?"

"She's fine, thank you."

"Do I call the *agents*—?"

"Later. Take your time if you must."

He would have liked to go after Kronin then and there, but he couldn't risk losing the girl, either by leaving her with the Frenchman or taking her to attack the other chartered boat. He urged the girl down to the cove where her beached sailboat waited. No one else was in sight.

"Can you tow the boat back?" he asked Jean. "I won't be coming back with you."

"She stays with you?" Jean had been admiring Gabriella from the first moment. "You have all the luck, dad."

Far out on the ruffled waters of the bay he saw a motor cruiser speed back toward the distant Riviera quai they had started from. It was Karl Kronin in retreat. But Durell knew that this was only a temporary victory. He would meet Kronin again. Next time Kronin would be far more dangerous.

When he had helped Jean shove off and fix a towline to the sloop, he returned to the girl. "Let's find O'Malley," he said quietly. "And you can tell me why you're so important that people want to kill you."

A road led from the deserted villa toward the trailer camp, a mile away. The girl was silent, her fine hands clenched in the pockets of her slacks. She had the clear olive skin of the Sicilian, but somewhere in her ancestry there was a hint of Norman conquerors, perhaps even a little Greek from ancient times. She had regained her composure. It did not surprise him, since her work as a trapeze artist kept her in daily touch with danger. Her nerves were good. And now that her fear was conquered, she spoke with a quiet, throaty accent he found enchanting.

"But I am not important at all," she explained. "Not to anyone. Oh, to my family, Pietro and Giovanni, in the circus. My cousins, I must explain. Otherwise, the Vanini family is almost died out except for Vecchio Zio."

"Who is he?"

" 'Old Uncle,' everyone calls him. He is in Sicily. You must understand, I have been with the circus all my life, born in a tent, trained to the work and to the wandering existence. Always it has been a living from —how do you say?—hand to mouth. But except for my work on the wire and with the horses, I am important to no one."

"O'Malley thinks otherwise. How did you meet?"

"The circus was in Las Vegas, touring America. He came to our little performance for—kicks, is it? And he waited to see me. Julio, my nephew, tried to keep him away. But somehow—he has a charming personality, do you not think?—I went to dinner with him. He seemed nice. He looks like Frank Sinatra, do you know? And with the same first name. He said he was just back from Vietnam. He had much money and he let me gamble in his establishment—oh, not much, for fun, he said. I—I had never visited such a place before. Or eaten so well. We—we had a good time." Her mouth curved in a small, reflective smile. "I like him very much, this man O'Malley."

"He fell in love with you," Durell stated.

"I do not know. With O'Malley you never know. He says little of what is truly in his heart."

"But you saw him again?"

"He insisted. Every night as long as we performed in Las Vegas. Julio, Giovanni—they were very disturbed. They want to keep me in the circus, of course. I do not blame them. Without me it would be noth-

72

ing." She made it a simple statement of fact. "It was a time of wonder for me, with O'Malley. My life has been very sheltered. There was much argument afterward about O'Malley. But——he was a member of the Fratelli della Notte. So they were afraid to object too loudly."

"Simply because he was a Brother?"

"But that is natural," she said.

"And you? Are you in love with O'Malley?"

"I do not know. I do not approve of myself in this fashion. It is disturbing. My life was uncomplicated until O'Malley interfered. Is that so hard to understand?"

"Not at all."

"Then, of course, I am not so free of guilt in my blood, either. Vecchio Zio, you see——" She paused and walked along with her head bowed in thought. "When I was just a little girl learning to be a bareback rider, they took me to see him. He sent for me. And when he sends for someone, you go. You obey. You do not deny him."

"Why not? He's just your old uncle—"

She looked shocked. "But I thought you knew. I thought O'Malley told you."

"We didn't have time to work it out."

"Oh!" She put a hand to her mouth, appalled. "Then, I can say nothing more."

"Gabriella, this is no time to be silent. Someone wants your life, and you must be important in some way. Things are not as simple as you'd like them to be. You're not a little girl now. Your life will never be simple or sheltered again."

She turned to him with tear-filled eyes. "Must it be so? You think I am callous because two men were just killed and I do not go all feminine and break down? I have seen much death and much killing. And I remember O'Malley and our week in Las Vegas with much tenderness. But I also remember Vecchio Zio, when I was such a child and they took me to see him. I know he has watched over me all my life. I have felt his presence everywhere, protecting me. But everything changed since I met O'Malley. Zio's presence is gone. No, not gone. Changed. He no longer loves me."

73

Her manner was charming and simple. Durell said, "Because of the men I had to kill just now?"

"Yes. And other things." She halted again, and her face was anguished. "Do you not understand? O'Malley is as good as being a dead man now."

They were near the trailer camp. It was set in a narrow notch of the steep promontory. The colorful tents and aluminum trailers, with little national flags from Germany, Scandinavia, Switzerland, and the Lowlands fluttering from television antennae and clothes lines, made it a minor United Nations in the sun of the Côte d'Azur. Durell could guess what O'Malley had done. He had rented a caravan and lost himself in the organized confusion of the campsite. It was a good place to hide. But Durell saw dangerous flaws in it. There was only one access road to the ochre-colored village on the Lower Corniche some miles away. The only other escape hatch had to be by boat.

He paused. "Which trailer is O'Malley's?"

"I do not know. He said he would watch for me."

"We'll wait here, then. In plain sight."

"Is that not dangerous? Those men—"

"They're gone. For the moment, anyway."

Durell was pleased that she showed no panic. He felt a quick admiration for her. She was a remarkable person, one of those rare individuals who make those around them feel happy and better simply by their presence. He listened to a thick quarrel in German, a song in French; he watched an incredible Swedish bikini walk toward the little trailer beach. Children played in the tidy camp streets.

"Tell me about the time you were taken to Vecchio Zio as a child. What do you remember of it?"

"Oh, it was such a strange place. Sicily is a poor land, but Zio lived like a feudal lord. There was a regular castle, as if in a fairy tale, you know? The men who escorted me were very respectful; but I was too young to know what Zio really meant to them."

"And just what was that?"

"I can never forget him." Gabriella smiled softly. "He

74

was so terrifying, so incredibly old. An old man with fearful flashing eyes, sitting in a big black chair like a throne, in a room with stone walls and a stone floor. They pushed me into the room and backed out and closed the door, and I was alone with him. He called me to come closer. It was the longest walk I ever remember, across a big carpet. I remember his hands—so white, the fingers like bones, and he had a big ring of black stone on his middle finger. It was a very old ring, older than Vecchio Zio. He asked me if I was afraid of him, and I said no, he was my uncle, and why should I be afraid of my uncle? He said I was a good child and he loved me and I was the last of the true blood line and many things I did not understand then. He said he would watch over me always and see that my life was happy and undisturbed. He showed me jewels in a carved box and silk and velvet dresses, and asked if I would like to live with him. A circus life, like gypsies, he said, was not fit for me, and that I must come and live with him."

"And you refused?"

"I burst into tears. I did not want to leave the Vanini family. And I did not want to live in that gloomy castle with that pale old man."

"Was he angry?"

"Oh, no. But disappointed. If I ever needed anything I was to come and ask for it, and he would give it to me at once."

"Did you ever see Vecchio Zio again?"

"No."

"You never asked for his help in anything?"

"No."

"Then, you don't even know if he's still alive. If he were, you wouldn't be in such danger now, would you?"

She traced a pattern in the soft sand with her toe. "He is alive. I think sometimes he will never die, because he is the Eldest Brother of the Fratelli della Notte."

Durell saw O'Malley plod down the camp street toward them. O'Malley looked thin, his straw hair in a cowlick. He wore a nylon shirt of dark blue, flapping about his hips, and khaki slacks. Behind him, like a patient water buffalo, was Bruno Brutelli, scowling in the sun. Nearby, like a military flanker, came Joey Milan, thin and ratty and suspicious.

"Gabriella, you made it!" O'Malley looked at Durell. "You're pretty good, Cajun. How'd you make it here?"

"You left some unfinished business in Switzerland." Durell put on his sunglasses. "You left a man named Dugalef, and I put a hole in him. You don't have to worry about Amos Rand any more. Dugalef killed him."

O'Malley scowled. "Rand was a foul-up. I'm not sorry. But what about your Colonel Mignon? Did he—?"

"He's dead, too."

O'Malley regarded him blandly. "And you think I chickened out, huh? But I thought it all over. This Kronin scares me, I admit. And I mean to save my own skin now. I'm in too deep to back out now, but I figured I'm more concerned about Gabriella than anything else. So maybe, I thought, I'd be better off working my way out of this alone. I still think I'm right about that." He kissed the girl. She stood remotely, a faint blush under her olive skin. "You look upset, Gabe. How did the Cajun find you?"

"He saved my life." She told O'Malley in simple words what had just happened, and her eyes searched his gaunt face as if looking for something she desperately needed and was not sure she could find. "I believe Durell will help you. But what you asked me over the telephone, O'Malley—I cannot do it. You made an enemy of Zio, and I will not help you against him."

"Baby, I'm not against *him*. It's Kronin. And now Kronin is after you, too, thanks to my stupidity and to the Cajun coming into it."

"You disobeyed and now you are in trouble," she said adamantly. "They will never forget or forgive you."

"Gabriella—"

"Let's get to the trailer," Durell suggested. He felt

76

uneasy in the open. "Gabriella, you should hear O'Malley out, at least."

She hesitated. Then she accepted his advice, where she had refused O'Malley's.

O'Malley did not like it.

THE trailer was a converted Renault truck, furnished with minimum economy. Joey Milan stood outside on guard while Brutelli headed at once to the small gas stove, where he had some pots simmering. Bruno's bulk was surprisingly deft in the narrow cooking area. He was chopping basil and had a shelf of herbs ready for a pasta he was preparing, together with a pungent chunk of fresh Tellegio cheese. Coffee simmered on a propane burner, and a bottle of Stravei vermouth stood on a shelf with bourbon and Scotch. O'Malley poured bourbon for Durell and Stravei for the girl.

"You both need something," O'Malley said.

"We need information, and fast," Durell told him.

O'Malley's grin was strained. "If I'd listened to your Grandpa Jonathan when we were kids, I'd never have gone in for a life of crime, fun, and games."

"Was Dugalef a Brother?" Durell asked flatly.

"One of the new ones. A grease man. I told you how everything was changed when I got back from Vietnam. New faces, new orders. Gabriella, I know how you feel about Vecchio Zio—he's like a wizard godfather to you. Okay. But just the same, he's the Eldest Brother, so the changes must have come on his orders, right?"

"It cannot be so," Gabriella protested.

"Look, I don't excuse myself or the Fratelli. We skate on thin ice all the time. But I've never been on ice. With me, gambling is a way of life. I couldn't stop any more than I could quit breathing. So the Fratelli financed me for a chip of the action. Like a bank, you know? We got along fine until the Army shipped me home after I was zapped in the jungle and I found out what the new bosses were doing. It was nothing you could prove. Just pieces here and there. Like traces of the Congs in the jungle. A smell in the air. Cops like Rand wouldn't cry if they found me in the gutter, but just the same—" O'Malley paused, uncomfortable. "I couldn't let these new people go on and cream our country. That's all there is to it. Maybe I was a damned fool; I owed nothing to anybody—"

"The whore with a heart of gold," Durell said.

O'Malley smiled crookedly. "Is patriotism a dirty word these days, Cajun?"

"You don't have to be ashamed of it."

"I'm only ashamed of getting me and Gabriella in this rat's corner right now. Listen, I've got a bit more than I gave you about the odd jobs that Kronin planned to do—surveying defense plants, reservoirs, power stations. I'll give it to you now. It's not enough, but it's all I got."

"And then what?" Durell asked.

O'Malley put an arm around Gabriella. "I got her into this; I've got to get her out. Kronin wants her now. We both led Kronin here, to her. I can't let him touch her, you understand?"

"What do you have in mind?"

O'Malley looked at Gabriella. She sat on a bunk with her hands folded in her lap. Her olive face told Durell nothing; her eyes watched O'Malley.

"It's up to her," O'Malley said.

"Why?"

"Because of Zio. The old uncle, her fairy godfather, like. He's king. His word is law to the Fratelli. So he's got to know what's been happening."

"Don't you believe he knows already?"

Gabriella shook her head and looked down at her folded hands. "He would not allow anyone to try to kill me. Unless—something has happened to him."

"Could he be dead?"

"I think not. I—I would somehow know it." She paused. "Vecchio Zio cannot be aware of what is happening."

Durell looked at O'Malley. "If there's no word in the Fratelli of changes in command, then we have to assume that some other group has managed to run things in the name of Vecchio Zio. He may be willingly helping them, of course—"

"No," Gabriella said firmly. "Not in this."

"Then Kronin may have him a prisoner and may be issuing orders in his name?"

"How can that be?" O'Malley asked.

"I don't know. We'll go and find out."

"Where?"

"To Sicily. Gabriella will show us the way. She's probably the only person who knows where to find him." Gabriella put a startled hand to her mouth. He added, "That's why you're so important. That's why Kronin wants to kill you. Maybe the old man doesn't know what's really happening. You'll have to tell him."

She was appalled. "In Sicily?"

"Yes."

O'Malley spoke quietly. "When do we go?"

"We'll start tonight," Durell said.

Arnie Thompson flew down from his Resident's office in Geneva Central that afternoon. Durell gave him the balance of O'Malley's notes, but the bald, craggy man looked with disfavor at O'Malley, who played solitaire with tireless fingers in the crowded trailer. Bruno was cooking again. Joey Milan was outside on watch in the campsite.

Gabriella wanted to return to the circus to say goodbye to her relatives, and Durell flatly refused. She was tearful. "But they cannot perform without me! They will be like lost children!"

"You have a greater responsibility just now. I know you don't like it, but we have to go ahead."

Durell asked Thompson for transportation on K Section funds. Thompson made no comment on the scrawled notes O'Malley had produced.

"You'll need more men, but I haven't any to spare for this assignment. The FBI—"

"I don't need any men. I've got them."

"These three?"

"These three sinners," said Durell. "A gambler, an ex-wrestler and collector for the mob, and a perjured jockey. And Gabriella, who has no faults at all. I think they'll do all right."

"Amateurs, against Kronin's people?"

"They have special talents."

Thompson shrugged. "I'll make the arrangements."

They flew from Nice to Rome that night, and checked in at the Vittoria, after a long taxi ride from the Leonardo da Vinci Airport. The hotel was around the corner from the Via Veneto. The Borghese Gardens were beaded with brilliant traffic lights pouring through the Pincio Gate in the old Roman wall. As far as Durell knew, no one had followed them from the airport.

He unpacked and ordered bourbon for himself and Cora Stravei for Gabriella from the bar downstairs and then telephoned to Rome Central, which was located over a bookstore on the busy Corso. Deirdre Padgett was stationed in Rome. The thought of seeing Deirdre cheered him. But the field chief laconically told him that Deirdre was in Munich. She was not expected back for several days.

As he hung up, the connecting door opened, and Gabriella entered his room. She wore a pink robe and had taken down her long, lustrous hair, and her face was scrubbed clean of all cosmetics. She looked vulnerable, like a child just after her evening bath. Her eyes were sympathetic.

"Is this—this Deirdre your girl?"

"How do you know?"

"I could tell by your voice. And I see you are disappointed. You had hoped to see her here?"

"You shouldn't eavesdrop . . . But she might have been able to help us."

Gabriella sighed and looked out over the Borghese Gardens from Durell's balcony. The night was balmy. Despite the late hour—it would soon be dawn—the roar of traffic from the Via Veneto had not abated.

"I wish I knew the true meaning of love," she said. "I do not know what it is. I do not think I can tell if I am in love or not."

"With O'Malley?"

"He—he is different, for me. Yet he is not a good man. Long ago I promised myself I would never marry. But many young girls tell themselves so, wishing independence, and change quickly when they mature. Sometimes I feel most confused. So I hid myself, as always, with the Vanini family."

"Your name is Vanini, but you speak of them as if they were not really related to you."

"Well, they never have told me who or what I truly am. The only thing I know is that Zio is my great-great uncle."

"With luck, we'll see him soon—with your help."

"But I cannot really help you." She regarded him with great dark eyes. "I have been trying to remember the exact way. We were in Palermo, but I was so young! It was after the war—I do not remember it, of course— but everything was in ruins. No food, few cars. But one was procured for me, a great black machine with vases of flowers inside. We drove for a long time. It was summer, very dusty, very dry. I always remember summers in Sicily."

"Can't you remember the way you went?"

She smiled ruefully. "I was such a little girl. I slept for a long time on the way."

Durell felt dismay. "Gabriella, do you mean you can't recall how to find Vecchio Zio's headquarters?"

"I am *trying!*" she said tightly. "But it does not come to me."

"But everyone thinks you can. O'Malley and the people who came after you on the Riviera."

"That is what is so terrible about it. They want something I cannot give."

He wondered if she were lying. Maybe so, through fear, but he didn't think this would be her motive. She was a girl who'd do what she thought right, whatever her terrors.

Taxi horns blared in the narrow street below his

window. Someone knocked, and he called to the boy to come in. But it was O'Malley with his bourbon and Stravei. O'Malley grinned and waved the bottles, then stood still as he saw Gabriella's slender figure at the balcony window.

"I intercepted the kid with the bottles, Sam. But I didn't know you were entertaining my girl."

Gabriella said, "I am *not* your girl, O'Malley."

"You will be, honey, unless the Cajun cuts my time. That wouldn't be very good."

"You're jumpy," Durell said. "We were just discussing how to find this place she was taken to as a child."

"What's the problem?"

"I cannot remember the road," Gabriella said thinly. "And you are—presumptuous, O'Malley. Just because you and I went to dinner a few times—"

"You never forgot those evenings, sweetheart, and you never will." O'Malley ripped the cap off the bourbon with an angry gesture. "Cajun, don't cut in on me."

Durell ignored him. "Gabriella, why did you come with us, unless you knew something that could help?"

"It is not something. It is someone. The Contessa Serafina Cimadori. A very great and powerful lady. She is most unusual, very high in the Fratelli della Notte. She is the one who escorted me to Vecchio Zio."

"Is she still alive?"

"I do not know. But I know where to find her. I remember that place clearly enough." She smiled dimly. "I remember it because of her son, a little boy, all pimples, not much older than I. He was cruel and very superior and nasty to me. Adolfo Cimadori, that was his name." She smiled again secretively. "It will be interesting to see what sort of a man Adolfo grew into."

"And where do we find Contessa Cimadori?"

"In Naples," she said. "It is, after all, on our way to Sicily."

They slept until early afternoon, then took the *rapido*

down the coast to Naples. The day was warm. Now and then from the clean train windows they glimpsed the blue Mediterranean. O'Malley had lapsed into a sullen silence. Bruno grumbled about the need to shop for special groceries he wanted to try in his cooking. Joey Milan's wizened face was, as always, remote and suspicious.

Durell had reserved seats, and no one seemed interested in them. Yet he had the feeling that ever since Nice they had not gone unobserved. Someone was watching them. Kronin wanted to stop Gabriella from reaching Vecchio Zio, and anything Kronin wanted to prevent was a sure sign that they should proceed on the same course.

They arrived in Naples a little after three, checked their luggage in the big, noisy terminal, shook off the shoals of self-appointed guides, pimps, peddlers, and urchins, and took a taxi to the Via Partenope on the bay front. The traffic had thickened incredibly since his last visit here. It took almost an hour, by way of narrow streets, to pass the Hotel Vesuvio and the Express office and reach the Parco Vittorio Emanuel. Gabriella explained that the contessa lived in an old palazzo on the Riviera di Chiaia, near the Piazza Vittoria.

"Pretty," O'Malley grunted, craning to stare at Vesuvius, crowned with smog beyond the blue bay.

"Look again," Durell said grimly. "We're being followed. The second cab behind us."

They passed Theresa Barra's, where he had once bought himself a dozen Italian silk neckties and a dozen pairs of gloves for Deirdre. The second taxi had now moved up directly behind them on the wide boulevard. He could not see the passengers. It could be a coincidence. The sun on the bay made little impression on the brooding mass of the Castel d'Ovo, with its yacht basin and tourist cafes under bright awnings.

"Stop at the next corner," he told the driver.

"But we are not there yet," Gabriella protested.

"We walk the rest of the way."

He stood on the pavement and watched the other cab glide by. Two men sat in the back, talking with Neapolitan animation. Neither looked his way. The taxi continued on up the waterfront boulevard and passed out of sight.

Durell ordered Bruno and Milan to stay on the narrow street that opened into the Piazza Vittoria. Number 22 was a faded palazzo with *trompe-l'oeil* painting on the ochre-plastered facade. There were heavy double doors with polished brass handles and peeling brown paint on the panels. The windows were shuttered against the spring sunlight. An air of decay shrouded the place, and the coat-of-arms with complex quarterings over the doorway had been chipped by bullets during the Nazi occupation. It looked as if it might fall on the heads of passersby at any moment.

"What do you want me to do?" O'Malley asked.

"Find the back way and get inside. Take your time. I'll meet you in there."

"I don't like it. Don't you trust Gabriella?"

"I don't trust anyone."

"Man, like you've changed since we were kids."

"We're not kids any more," Durell said. "And we're not playing cops and robbers. Just do as I say."

O'Malley relaxed with a visible effort, then patted Gabriella's shoulder and went to seek an alley in the rear. The girl watched him go and said, "He is so strange. I do not understand him."

"He loves you, but there's a flaw in the picture."

"And what is that?"

"He doesn't admit knowing the word 'love.' "

"I do not understand you, either."

"You don't have to," Durell said.

He considered the big knocker on the door, then tried the bronze handles. The door was not locked, which surprised him and then worried him. You lock your doors in Naples or lose your shirt.

He went in first. And again was surprised. The facade of the palazzo was grimy and decayed, but the tiny court within was a rich, carefully polished jewel, beautiful with bright sunlight and shadow. There was a fountain of green-veined marble, gay flower beds, a waterfall of wisteria from a balcony ahead. Wrought-iron chairs were disposed around a blue umbrella in a square iron table. A shell path made further arabesques on the ground, and a palm tree leaned gracefully from one side of the court.

"Do you remember this, Gabriella?"

"Yes, it comes back to me. Nothing is changed."

"Fine. Stay close beside me."

"Can there be danger here?" she asked.

"Anywhere."

The interior windows over the court were hidden by drawn draperies. A scent of flowers filled the air. No one was in sight. An open door beckoned ahead. Inside, the hallway was furnished with cool but dusty antiques and a silk rug. He saw himself in a Venetian mirror at the foot of a delicate, curving staircase—

"S-sst!" someone said.

Durell turned, a hand on the gun in his pocket, Gabriella made a small sound of surprise.

"Adolfo! Adolfo, is it you?"

The man came forward as gracefully as a dark flower blown by the wind. His smiled showed capped teeth.

"It is Gabriella? *Cara* Gabriella!" He wore a fawn-colored coat with a mauve scarf at his throat, gray Daks and pointed, gleaming Italian shoes. "Gabriella, my childhood darling, I would know you anywhere! How often have I sighed in my dreams for you!" His snicker made the remark obscene.

Gabriella halted. Her manner cooled. "You have not changed much, Adolfo."

"Ah, but I am a grown man now."

"Still devoted to the contessa?"

"*Mamina* is a remarkable woman."

"True. We have come to see her."

"I know, I know. We have been waiting."

Adolfo Cimadori slid dark, liquid eyes toward Durell's tall form. His brows looked plucked, and his black hair was brushed sleekly to his long, aristocratic head. "We have been waiting for Signor Durell, too. Come this way, *carissima*."

"One moment," Durell said.

Adolfo smiled. "You are surprised? But in this modern world should one more miracle startle you? You see how well I speak English, *si*? One day I shall go to New York. To open a branch office, so to speak."

"Who told you we were coming?" Durell asked.

"Does it matter? We know. Eyes and ears are everywhere. The miracle of today. But I cannot linger. It devastates me. I will wait here for when the contessa refuses you. Then I may be able to help. Gabriella, I would *like* to help. For old time's sake, as you might say."

Gabriella was bewildered. "But the contessa cannot even know what we wish to ask of her."

"She knows. She thinks of you as a naughty little girl." Adolfo Cimadori rolled his eyes. "But I think of you as—ah, you have changed, become so beautiful!"

"Snake!" she snapped. "You are still the same little snake you were long ago."

"You will change your mind. But hurry! The contessa does not like to be kept waiting. You remember her room? She changes nothing. Go. You will see me again before you leave."

Gabriella was pale as they mounted the stairs. Looking back, Durell saw that Adolfo had silently vanished. Kronin was brilliant at his work. He had guessed why Durell had taken Gabriella with him and just as easily guessed their destination. So there could be no element of surprise now, he thought grimly. Everything was uphill, as usual. Every move they made was known, countered, and sidetracked.

"He had loathsome pimples," Gabriella murmured. "They are gone now, but it is as if I can still see them."

"What is he after?"

She shrugged. "He was a vicious, greedy boy. The man will be no better."

The gilt doors at the end of the upper hall were open. Durell felt as if it might be an execution chamber. But there was no one in the room except Contessa Serafina Cimadori.

And where her son, Adolfo, had seemed the very

incarnation of degenerate evil, she was outwardly the precise opposite. He knew at once she had been a great lady, born to aristocracy, intelligent and gracious. An ornate tea service waited for them on a polished table, together with bottles of whiskey, Scotch, Campari, gin, and vermouth. Carved, gilded cupids smiled at them from every corner of the big room.

"Gabriella, my dear, dear child."

"Contessa Serafina . . ."

"You are more beautiful than it was reported. How many tears I have shed, thinking of your wasted life!"

"It has not been wasted, my contessa."

"You could have lived with me and had everything. Everything! But you chose to stay with that foolish, pitiful little circus, the Vanini family—"

"It was my choice."

"Yes. And Zio ordered it so." The woman turned her proud head toward Durell. "And this is your new friend? It is Mr. Durell who persuaded you to come here on such a foolish mission! Is he your lover?"

Gabriella was shocked. "No, Contessa."

"He is a dangerous man. Perhaps a cruel one. You conceal your surprise very well, Mr. Durell."

"Nothing surprises me now, Contessa," he said politely. He kept Gabriella and himself out of the line of fire from the open doors to this lovely room. "Nothing except possibly women."

"You lie gracefully. You know women better than most. Am I beautiful, Signor Durell?"

"Yes," he said truthfully.

He knew she was old enough to be Gabriella's mother. But now and then he'd met women who seemed immortal in their feminine beauty. There was pride in her fine, tilted head, the careful blonde hair done in a regal coronet, the slim, tanned arms, the good legs. She was that famous combination of ancient Norman blood and local noble stock, reflected in her dark eyes, which contrasted with her hair. Her mouth was full and sensuous. She wore a Pucci frock that accented a figure still firmly curved.

She smiled as he appraised her, and her eyes were

as bold and objective as his own. "You will have bourbon, I think, Signor Durell. And you, Gabriella? Stravei?"

"Nothing, thank you," the girl whispered.

"Then come and kiss me, my dear."

Gabriella obeyed dutifully, with just a twinge of reluctance.

"You have indeed grown beautiful, poor girl," Contessa Serafina murmured. "Zio would be delighted to see you."

"Then you will take us to see him?"

The contessa looked at Durell. "Why have you brought this child to me? Why do you wish to see Zio?"

"It's urgent enough," Durell said.

"But I cannot give permission so casually. No one sees Zio. He is most—secluded. You understand, it is astonishing—no, dismaying—that you even know of his existence. It cannot be permitted, such knowledge."

"We must see him," Durell insisted.

"And you use Gabriella for your ends? We know all about you, Signor Durell. And while our main opponents"—she smiled—"are the police, we are surprised that a man in your position, with your duties, shows interest in us."

"The interest was forced upon me."

"By petty thieves!" For the first time there was a touch of steel behind the beautiful, throaty voice. "By traitors who betray their vows, by scum, the sweepings of the gutter."

Gabriella broke in. "But O'Malley is not—"

"Ah, poor Gabriella."

"Please stop calling me that," she said.

"But you are a child, you have been protected all your life, and you do not know what these men have persuaded you to do. And you, Mr. Durell, at such risk to this girl and yourself, have not answered me as to why you seek Zio."

"We just want to talk to him."

"Of what?"

"Of certain changes in the Fratelli della Notte."

"You should not even mention the name. Not here or anywhere. It is foolhardy."

Gabriella spoke in a burst of passion. "But Vecchio Zio would never harm me!"

"Of course not, you lovely child."

"Then you must take me to see him, Contessa. Or at least you must tell me the way."

"It is impossible."

"I remember the place!"

"You cannot, or you would not ask my help."

Gabriella clenched her small fists. "But Zio said that if I ever needed him, no matter when or where, I was to come to him, from anywhere in the world, at any time."

"You sound desperate about this. But is it not merely to help this man, this Durell, who you must know is an American intelligence agent."

"No."

"Durell could bring much trouble to Zio."

"He would not."

"You are naive. And have you considered, dear child," the contessa said gently, "that Zio may no longer wish to see you?"

"But he promised!" Gabriella cried.

"He made a fond and sentimental speech to a lovely child. But you are a woman now and you may put him in danger. So I must tell you that Vecchio Zio forbids you to come. More than that, he has ordered us to prevent it by any means. By *any* means, do you understand?" Contessa Serafina Cimadori smiled sadly. "Such a blow to you. I can see it. But you must go home, my dear. At once. Otherwise . . . we must kill you."

13 • • • • • •

SOMEWHERE in the exquisite palazzo a canary began to trill mindlessly up and down the scale. The warm Neapolitan sunlight shafted through the tall windows and touched the woman's blonde, elegant head, the rich Aubusson rug, the paintings in ornate frames on the wall. Durell could hear the fountain tinkling in the courtyard garden below the windows.

He watched Gabriella go pale and touch her heart as if she had been struck in the breast. She looked like someone who had just been stripped naked in a cold and bitter world, left vulnerable and alone to face an awful disillusionment. How many years had she lived, he wondered, with the warm security of knowing that someone incredibly powerful in secret ways watched over her like some ancient wizard, aware of all she did, guarding and comforting her? To Gabriella, Vecchio Zio must have seemed all-powerful, remote, but still intensely personal, always involved with her welfare.

With just a few words Contessa Serafina had stripped her of the foundations of her world, which seemed so sure ever since that fairy-tale day when she was taken as a child to this mysterious source of power, wisdom, and strength. With those words the contessa had also stripped herself of her facade of patrician elegance. Cruelty grated in her voice, and a savage triumph, and her beautiful face hardened into an adamantine mask.

She was an enemy, Durell thought, who would not be easy to cope with. He broke the deathly silence.

"I don't believe you, Contessa."

91

She smiled graciously. "And just what don't you believe, Signor Durell?"

"Zio would not refuse to see Gabriella. We want to hear it directly from him."

"Impossible."

"We intend to see him. We ask your help again."

Her laugh was scornful. "You ask my suicide. I am not really so important. There are others who have much greater influence—"

"Such as Karl Kronin?" he asked easily.

Her eyes were a blank dark blue, like closed convolvulus flowers. "I do not know the name." She stood up with splendid grace, hands clasped before her. "Mr. Durell, you are in a world you cannot comprehend, one that has existed for many centuries. What do you know about the Fratelli? We rob, yes. We commit crimes, yes. But we also do much, much good. We exist because we are a historical necessity. Oppression called us into being, and we survive one way or another until history calls us again. During the Nazi occupation of Italy we formed an underground and fought as a resistance movement for patriotism. We hated Mussolini, we hated the Nazis. Many of the Brothers died for Sicily. And when your Allied troops invaded the island, who greeted them and acted as eyes and ears against the Tiger tanks? Who directed your Naval fire on enemy divisions that might have bathed your landing beaches in blood? The Fratelli della Notte was there, Mr. Durell. When the people of Naples rose up against the Nazis who shot and killed us, we fought with what we had— the knife, poison, gun, the dynamite."

The woman paused, panting with her emotion. Her great eyes were alight with passion. "So now we exist in crime. We must exist somehow. We are not related to the Honored Society, what you call the Mafia. What we did is not recorded. We asked for no thanks. But we go on. We still keep people alive with food and money and all sorts of help—"

Durell deliberately looked about the exquisite room. "Yes. And you have done well by it."

She dismissed the palazzo with a wave of her hand.

"It does not belong to me. It is all for Vecchio Zio."

"Has he ever come here?"

"Of course not."

"Has he ever left Sicily?"

"There is no need," she snapped, and then she bit her lip. "Ah, you are a clever man, infuriating me."

"So he's still alive and still in Sicily."

"You will never, never find him," she said.

"We'll see." He held out a hand for Gabriella, who had stood like stone ever since the contessa pronounced what might be her death sentence. "Come along. There's nothing for us here."

No one interfered as they went down the curving steps. The doors to the courtyard were still open, bright with sunshine and flowers. An orange butterfly floated from the wisteria to the fountain and back again.

Then Adolfo Cimadori appeared from a doorway at their back, swaying like a tall dark blossom in the wind.

"S-sst!" He winked, exaggeratedly conspiratorial. Durell halted. Gabriella would have gone on, her head high, but Durell checked her.

"What is it, Adolfo?" she asked.

"I promised help. I knew you would need it. Carissima, you look as if you have seen a ghost." Adolfo giggled. "We must speak softly. Mamina would be very angry if she knew I spoke to you. She thinks I have gone out."

"Well?" Durell asked.

"You want help, do you not? The contessa turned you down, as I knew she would. Why should she disobey orders? She loves her luxury. She is clever but not more clever than I. Me, I am a greedy man."

Durell waited. Adolfo elaborately fitted a cigarette into a black holder and lit it with a gold lighter. He did not inhale. He puffed and blew the smoke awkwardly.

"I need money," he said.

"How much?"

"We can discuss it at my apartment. It is a very private place, one I keep for myself, for my true life.

Do you think I enjoy being a little boy at the beck and call of my mother? I have gone into—ah—business for myself. In a small way."

"You don't pay tribute to the Fratelli?"

Adolfo smiled and waved his cigarette like a baton. "All Americans are so blunt. But this is a very dangerous matter. I take a great risk simply speaking to you. But I can direct you to Zio."

Gabriella spoke at last. "He would not allow a man like you in his sight," she said flatly.

Adolfo flushed, and cold hatred flashed in his eyes. Then he shrugged. "Gabriella, you have always disliked me. A pity, since we could have been such good friends. Perhaps I will not help you, after all. Why should I? It is too great a risk. No, no, I have changed my mind. *Ciao.*"

Durell crossed the terazzo floor and caught the man's blue scarf in his fist. "You said you were greedy, Adolfo. How greedy?"

Adolfo licked his lips. "Blunt, yes. Crude, yes. But rich. Like all Americans. I want a hundred thousand dollars."

"Impossible."

"Fifty, then."

"It depends on how valid your information proves."

"Twenty-five now, the balance when you return." Adolfo frowned. "No, that will not do. You may not return. So you must put the money in a bank for me, to be paid after a specific date."

"No. When we return. You could lie to us. You could walk us into a trap."

Adolfo smiled. "That is a chance you take. You are a gambler, no? And only I can help you. But not here, please. Mama will be down shortly to take the sun in the garden. At my apartment in two hours, yes?"

"Where?"

"Via Mirabella, forty-five, on Vomero Hill. You know it?"

"I know it."

"In two hours, then." Adolfo adjusted his rumpled scarf. "I will be waiting with all the information you need. Bring the money—as much money as you can. I need it, frankly. My tastes are most expensive."

Durell looked at him with open contempt. "It's a deal," he said quietly.

O'Malley came quickly toward him down the street, from the Riviera di Chiaia. His blond hair looked white in the hot Neapolitan sunlight. Traffic came and went with wild abandon. At the far corner, a narrow intersection, Joey Milan stood uncertainly near a wall.

Something had happened.

O'Malley was sweating when he joined them. "There was no way in through the back, Cajun. Glad you got out without trouble." He looked at Gabriella. "What's the matter?"

"We were turned down," Durell said shortly. "But it's not over yet. What's biting you?"

"Like that dumb Bruno, you know what he did?" O'Malley jammed angry hands in his pockets. "That stupid clod. He let them take him."

"Where?"

"He saw this *salumeria,* and you know how he is about food. He went to buy stuff for his goddam cooking. Wanted to make vermicelli a la putana. Says it's a speciality of Naples." He grinned. "A quick meal, originated while the ladies of pleasure waited for another trick. Anyway, Bruno went into this deli and didn't come out. Joey Milan thinks they took him."

"HOW long ago?" Durell asked.

"Four, five minutes."

Durell hid his immediate anxiety. He told O'Malley to go in the front way, with Milan to cover him. He himself would find the back door and enter that way.

"And Gabriella?"

"She comes with me," Durell said.

O'Malley didn't like it. "You're getting real possessive, Cajun. Gabriella is a real swinger, but she belongs to me."

"She belongs to all of us just now. And she's the one in the most danger. She stays with me, in the open."

O'Malley nodded reluctantly. It occurred to Durell that O'Malley's jealousy could turn into a real problem soon. But it had to wait. He went with the girl around the corner, through crowded streets. Traffic was heavy. There seemed to be nothing out of the ordinary in the scene.

Gabriella spoke quietly. "O'Malley is angry with you, Cajun. What is a 'swinger?' "

"A lovely and attractive girl."

"You think he regards me that way?"

"He's in love with you, Gabriella."

She was silent. Durell's mind was on the search for Bruno. What he had seen of the *salumeria* was not encouraging. A small shop with fly-specked windows hiding a variety of Neapolitan sausages, cheeses, and gaudy stacks of canned food. Halfway to the next street he saw the alley. It was just wide enough for a small black Fiat to be jammed between the blank walls of the adjacent buildings. Durell could not see beyond the little car. But vague movement stirred in the deep shadows where the sun never penetrated the alley. An orchestration of garbage smells struck him as he stepped in from the street. Gabriella stepped daintily behind him.

A radio blared, louder than usual, even for Naples. It drowned out all other sounds. He counted blank doorways and decided that it came from the rooms behind the *salumeria*. But there was no sign of violence, none of Bruno. Only the empty Fiat. It had been slammed into the wall of the opposite house, crumpling the fenders, but its engine still ran. Nobody was behind the wheel.

Durell took out his gun.

"What is it?" Gabriella whispered. "Is Bruno—?"

"I don't know yet. He's still around."

There was just space enough on the opposite side of the Fiat to squeeze through. He waved the girl back for a moment. Then he saw the man who sprawled in the filthy water in the center of the alley. He lay face down, his legs oddly splayed. One arm was broken. It was not Bruno. His face was just a face, narrow and ratty, with a look of surprise on its features. For a moment Durell thought he was dead. Then the man groaned in his unconsciousness.

The back door of the delicatessen was open. It looked as if someone had torn it off its hinges. A man sat there, crosswise, with a broken neck. Beyond, all was in darkness in a narrow hallway that seemed to lead nowhere.

"Bruno?" Durell called softly. There was no answer. He stepped over the dead man.

"Bruno?"

"Goddammit." Someone spoke in the black stifling hole. "I couldn't help it, Cajun. They tried to grease me."

Brutelli lurched into sight. He staggered, and his huge bulk caromed from one wall to the other. He held a wickedly glinting knife with the wide blade flat—the easier to slip between an opponent's ribs. His other arm was filled with a paper bag bulging with cans and packets of food.

97

His grin was amiable, almost joyous. "Frank is comin' along with Joey. Put away the heat, Cajun. It's all over."

"What happened to you?"

There was blood on Bruno's shirt and a cut over his eye. "Hell, there was only two of them." He stepped over the dead man in the doorway and eyed him objectively. "Broken neck, huh? I didn't mean to do *that*." He seemed surprised. "So they tol' me to come inna back room, like, to see some special goodies in the way of groceries, and I was dumb enough to go. They was waitin' in there. But they didn't figure on ol' Bruno. Even so, they almost suckered me into the car before I reasoned it out. I got a little mad."

"So I see." Durrell hid his vast relief. Bruno put away his knife and heaved his groceries into a more comfortable position in his massive left arm. "Come on, Frank. Let's go, Joey."

Out of the gloom came O'Malley and Milan. From beyond, muffled by the intervening walls to the *salumeria*, came a sudden spate of recrimination, a woman's angry voice, and the placating murmur of a man's reply.

"I'm ready," Bruno said amiably. "Let's find a place where I can cook this stuff."

They checked into a hotel near the Theresa Barra glove shop, since Durell felt uneasy about leaving his companions, and especially Gabriella, exposed temporarily on the open streets of Naples. An accident would be simple to arrange in the wild traffic along the Via Partenope. The bay never looked more beautiful or serene. Distant Capri loomed far off in the blue water, the height of Anacapri seeming to float in the incredible sky. The sidewalk cafes were crowded now, and among them were early-bird tourists, with their inevitable festoons of cameras, beating the summer crush.

The hotel apartment was small and dingy, but it seemed safe enough. It was three o'clock. Half an hour to his appointment with Adolfo Cimadori.

"You going alone?" O'Malley asked aggressively.

"Better that way. You three take care of the girl.

She's more important to us than Fort Knox."

"You trust that Adolfo flower?"

"No, but he's our only lead now."

"I am sorry," Gabriella apologized. "Perhaps if we went to Palermo and tried some of the roads, I would recognize them, and it might come back to me, the way to Vecchio Zio's place."

" 'Castle,' you said," Durell reminded her.

"Yes, an old Crusader or Norman ruin."

"Well, that may be a help. Only so many of them are still habitable." Durell frowned. "But Sicily is too big. It would take a long time to check them all out."

"I am so sorry. I—I wish I had not agreed to this. It was wrong of me. I was mistaken about Zio. I thought —hoped—he would see me at any time."

"Keep on believing it," Durell said.

"But these men who try to stop us—they must all take orders from Zio."

"I doubt it."

"It could not be otherwise," she objected. "Zio commands and Zio is obeyed."

"Maybe not this time."

But there was more on her mind. Durell was aware of it from the way she hovered near him, as if she were reluctant to stay with O'Malley. She bit her pink lip and made a little sound and traced a faded rose in the carpet with her foot, arching her toe like a ballerina. O'Malley, lounging in the kitchen doorway of the hotel apartment, glowered at her.

"What's bugging you, kitten?" he asked.

"Nothing, O'Malley. But I would feel safer—"

"With the Cajun?"

"Perhaps. Not that I reflect on you, but—"

"But he's getting to you, is that it?"

"O'Malley, you have no right to criticize me," she flared. "You have no claim on me."

"Oh, yes, I have, baby. Lots of claims." He twitched away from the door and crossed toward Durell. He walked like a fighter crossing a ring, his shoulders hunched. Attracted by the tightness of his voice, Bruno and Joey came to watch. All at once the atmosphere in the drab apartment was electric. "Cajun, are you playing for her?" O'Malley asked.

"No."

"She's my girl. You know that?"

Gabriella said in a small voice, "I am not your girl, O'Malley. I am free. I have always been free."

"You're not going with the Cajun."

It was an ultimatum, and Durell saw no profit in taking it up. O'Malley was too volatile. He reminded himself he was dealing with men who had no morality. Shrugging, he moved Gabriella toward the kitchen door.

"Go and help Bruno get his fancy dinner together, like a good girl. O'Malley is right. You're safer here. What I have to do now is better done alone."

"But they only want to lure you where they can kill you," she protested. "O'Malley, you should go with him."

"You certainly worry about the Cajun, don't you?" O'Malley asked angrily.

"I worry about all of us."

"Please do as I say," Durell told her.

Reluctantly she walked toward the kitchen. Bruno lumbered after her, and his voice made a low growl as they talked in there. Joey Milan picked up a deck of cards he had acquired somewhere and made thin riffling sounds as he shuffled them. His eyes never left Durell. O'Malley paced to the window and back, lean and dangerous. From the kitchen came a clatter of pots and pans. The sound eased him, and he laughed. "All right, Cajun, we won't knife each other about it, right? Just remember, she's my girl."

"If she says so."

"*I* say so. It's enough, right?" Some of the feral look left O'Malley's eyes. "So you go to that pink-pants Adolfo's place alone. But what if you don't come back? I've given you all I could get on Kronin and the Fratelli. Now I'm only interested in finding a way out for me and Gabriella. Any way, understand? On any terms. Maybe Joey and Bruno and I should've gone to Rio or somewhere and forgot the whole business." O'Malley swore softly. "I don't know how I ever got stupid enough to get on this patriotic kick in the first place."

Durell smiled. "We all have our neuroses."

He had a few minutes to spare. He walked in the sunshine of the Via Partenope, with the cone of Vesuvius looming in the distant haze across the Bay, and on impulse he turned into the Theresa Barra shop and asked an obliging clerk if he could use the telephone in the back room. They remembered him from his last visit, and he was waved on.

He called Naples Control and asked for Onan McElroy. He was in luck. Razzatti was on duty. Durell identified himself with the usual code phrase, and McElroy came on and told him he'd been alerted by Thompson in Geneva and what could he do now for him? Durell asked for a rundown on Adolfo Cimadori and the contessa, his mother, at once.

McElroy replied immediately. "He's no good, Cajun. The locals know all about him but haven't touched him yet because he's small dung. They want the Fratelli, too." The K Section man paused. "Is your phone safe?"

Durell looked through the doorway into the shop. It was empty except for two obviously innocent American tourists, buying gloves for the woman and a Borsalino hat for the man. "Yes, safe enough."

"Good. We know Adolfo's trying to break away from Mama's whip and set himself up as a *pezzo di novanta* —a big shot—in the narcotics business. It's a small operation, with a sideline in white slavery, what else? So the fuzz hasn't touched him. They want the contessa badly and hope the son will slip in the muck and give them the break they need. But Cajun, you're wading into deep and dirty waters."

"I know. What I want to learn is if Adolfo ever goes to Sicily—and when and where if he goes."

"Can do. Give me a bit of time."

"I'll call back," Durell said.

He hung up and thanked the clerk and walked around the corner, beyond the American Express office, crossed the Via Santa Lucia to the taxi stand opposite, and gave the villainous cab driver the address of Adolfo Cimadori at Via Mirabella, 45.

Sometimes you had no choice about the tools you used in the business, he reflected, and couldn't examine too much into their quality. Success was measured by accomplishment and survival. You paid any price for the first and often the second, too. Cruelty was a regular signpost in his shadow world. You had to sacrifice friends if it came to a choice. O'Malley suspected this. Even though there once had been a time when he'd known every vagary of O'Malley's temperament, he did not feel assured now. O'Malley was sulky, regretting the cause he had taken up. Durell didn't know how far he could trust O'Malley or the other two.

But Gabriella was different. She had a basic innocence that made her defenseless. She would grow up before this was ended, and the process would be most painful. Already, with the news that her fabled Zio refused to see her, she knew that her security had trembled and turned into a quagmire under her feet. He felt protective toward her, despite the rules he had to obey, and he knew he would defy those rules in order to see her safely through her coming ordeal.

The taxi halted, and the driver pointed to the address he wanted.

For Naples, it was a quiet street. The apartment house was new, built on the rubble of old devastation. It had a garden court with a long facade that faced the tilted uphill street. Concrete balconies were gay with laundry, like a display of flags. An arcade led into a central court, with a piece of concrete statuary as hideous and stupid as most of the undisciplined, phony work that passed as modern art. Children ran and screamed in the sunny corners of the court. Beyond was another entrance and a row of mailboxes with elegantly polished and engraved brass nameplates.

He found Cimadori's name under number 4C and pushed the bell. There was no elevator. He took the concrete staircase that angled up in a narrow shaft toward a skylight far above.

The afternoon was sultry, but it was cool in this rabbit warren. Originally there had been pretensions to elegance here, but the volatile Neapolitans had dulled this somewhat. At the fourth-floor landing he looked back and thought he saw a shadow move far below. But he wasn't sure and went on.

The door to 4C was locked. He rang and waited, rang again, then thought he heard the scrape of footsteps on the stairs. He walked back and looked down the shaft. Nothing. But he felt pretty sure now.

A fire exit led him onto the long balcony that overlooked the courtyard where the children played. Their screaming quarrels drifted up in distorted echoes. Durell walked along the balcony, counting windows under the slanted awnings that had been let down against the afternoon sun. It was the hour in Naples when shops closed and the long siesta took place, and Neapolitans hid from the day's heat.

He was sweating when he reached the right window, but it was not from the sun that cooked the concrete walls. The window he wanted was open. He stood there, wishing the children below would be silent for just a moment so he could listen better. But he could hear nothing inside Cimadori's apartment and moved in quickly, past the limp draperies, aware of his shadow shooting ahead to betray him. Danger waited here, but he could not guess where and when it might strike. He was familiar with this fear and considered the primordial tightening in his belly as natural and useful. It alerted his reflexes, and he did not let it stop him.

The room was empty, furnished in an Italian version of Danish modern, with elaborately slung canvas chairs, an orange couch under a big painting that was only a splash of disorienting color, a coffee table set with liqueurs, including one tall golden bottle of Strega. There was perfume in the air—and a smell of something else.

Durell crossed the room to a hall door beyond the foyer. The chain was not on. He turned the latch and put it on free but did not open it. Then he returned to the main room of the apartment.

"Adolfo?" he called quietly. He did not expect an

answer. But he got a small, muffled animal grunt from the next room.

This door was inches ajar. He pushed it open with the muzzle of his gun. He did not remember taking it from his underarm holster. The door was heavy. He pushed it silently open to reveal a bedroom with rich ornamentation and sumptuous silken hangings. The shutters were tightly closed, but a red-shaded lamp beside the huge swan bed cast a bloody glow over the gilt and silver room.

Adolfo lay on the bed in a foetal position, legs tight under his belly, his neck bent, one patent-leather shoe on the floor under his dangling feet. He wore a red silk jacket and an open silk shirt and dark slacks. In the middle of his shirt was an embellishment Adolfo Cimadori obviously had not wanted or expected. It was the jeweled, elaborate hilt of a knife. The ruby stone at the end of the grip was not as scarlet as the blood that flowed down his groin and stained the expensive coverlet of his swan bed.

The miracle was that he still lived.

His eyes were blind and black, and a long sigh came from his slack mouth as Durell moved nearer. He tried to say something, but it was only meaningless air. Durell did not touch him.

The air smelled of perfume, blood, and feces, which stained Adolfo's elegant slacks.

He moved around the bed and checked the bath, going fast; but he found only sunshine on a glittering tray of cosmetics. He repeated the careful, swift process with two closet doors. Nobody waited for him to turn his back.

He returned to the dying man. "Adolfo, can you hear me?"

The breath sighed with sibilance. *"Si . . ."*

"Who did it, Adolfo?"

He got a faint negative shake of the head. Adolfo drew his knees up tighter against the wound in his belly. There was grayness under his skin. In his eyes was defiance and even amusement.

"Can't you tell me?" Durell insisted.

"I could—but I—I will not," he gasped.

"I brought you the money. Twenty-five thousand American dollars."

"Leave it—beside me."

"But we made a bargain."

Petty avarice flickered in the dying eyes. *"Si."*

"Then tell me where to find Vecchio Zio." Durell was urgent. "Quickly."

"Would—would a *dottore* help me?"

"No."

"Zio—" There was a long pause. "Ah, it hurts!"

"Where can I find Zio?"

"He will—he will kill you."

"I don't believe that. He'll help Gabriella."

"No. Mama—spoke the truth."

Durell said: "The money is yours. Where is he?"

"Castel San Gi—Gi—"

There was a pause.

"Go on," Durell said thinly.

But he spoke to a dead man.

DURELL tore the room apart. He worked with efficient haste, rooting out every possible secret. But someone had been here before him. Someone who was almost as professional as he. He found nothing.

He searched the dead man, not moving him any more than necessary. He found nothing there, either. Then he returned to the brightly colored living room. The children still screeched and ran in the courtyard.

And Karl Kronin waited for him.

He was not surprised. He had expected it.

Kronin seemed bigger than life, a dark shadow that darkened all the gay plumage of Cimadori's cage. He was like an evil bird of prey, bald head shining, shoulders hunched, feet flat on the rug, in a dark suit, an immaculate white shirt, and a dark tie with a stone in it that winked like a third eye. The gaze was hooded and vulturine; but there was sensuality in the broad, thick lips. His voice was heavy and hoarse.

"Ah, Mr. Durell, such a disappointment. I must ask you not to shoot me out of hand. It would be a disaster for both of us. You may keep your gun on me, but do not use it yet, please." Kronin smiled with complete assurance.

Durell's finger had indeed tightened with temptation on the trigger of his gun. Here was the man who had tried to kill him; here was the murderer of blind Colonel Mignon and foolish Amos Rand. Kronin's only rule was gold and personal power and enjoyment of his role at the center of international affairs. Durell felt a dryness in his throat and hatred in his belly. But he could not afford to pull the trigger. Kronin was right.

The man's English was only slightly accented. "I have come to bargain with you, and you expected me, eh? So. If you shoot me now, your mission will—how do you say it?—go down the drain. So I weighed the risks. I am not more personally brave than the next man, but I know all about you, Mr. Durell. You are intelligent and dangerous. But intelligence comes first. May we talk for a few moments?"

"Did you kill Adolfo?" he asked.

"That piece of dung? Not I."

"Your men, then?"

"That is what they are paid for." Kronin's bald head was thrust even farther forward on his heavy shoulders. He was a powerful man, and Durell knew he wore a false left leg, although even when Kronin moved, ever so carefully under his gun, he scarcely betrayed his limp. It was said that Kronin lost the leg while fighting with the Albanian Reds against King Zog. But many things were said about Kronin, and no one could separate truth from the lies. All Durell knew at this moment was that he faced a man who was ruthless, amoral, and a Judas who would betray anyone for less than thirty pieces of silver. Kronin had almost put the fear of God into him. Now he had the hunter before him. It would be easy to kill him, Durell decided.

As if divining his thought, Kronin gestured for permission to sit down, hiked up his trouser leg with meticulous care, and showed a glint of aluminum from his false limb as he settled himself.

"We can come to terms of mutual profit," he said decisively. "I know you do not believe this, but if you hear me out, you will know I speak the truth. Otherwise, why should I take this dreadful risk of confronting you? We both know this world better than most. I admire you. I wish we could work together." He held up a placating hand against Durell's anger. "I do not seriously suggest this. I know your morality. But it is a pity, since we are more intelligent than most, and life could be full and rich for us if we could cooperate."

"There isn't room in the world for both of us," Durell said harshly.

"But you will listen?"

Durell nodded. "For a few moments."

"Good. As for what you seek here, you have lost it, as you know. A pity you found Adolfo dead, eh? He might actually have helped you, in his petty way."

So, Durell thought, *Kronin did not know that his assassin had slipped and left before making certain that Cimadori was actually dead. Kronin did not know that Adolfo had gasped out a few words before he died.* "Go on," he said.

"Adolfo was dirt, as I said. A foolish and dissipated young man, indulging in perverted luxuries. One cannot survive like a child playing with fire. No one will mourn him. How much money did he want?"

"Twenty-five thousand dollars," Durell said.

"And you brought it with you?"

"I have it, yes."

Kronin licked his wide lips. He looked more evil than ever. There was an instant hunger in him that he could not hide. "It is a small sum but tidy."

"Do you think you can get it from me?"

"Perhaps. Is it worth your life?"

"You're talking nonsense," said Durell.

"Then is it worth Gabriella's life? Because you are all dead, you know. Dead and not aware of it yet. You have no idea how we can wait, how patient we can be. A few months, some years, even twenty years. And you will be cruelly dead. The charming Gabriella will be first."

"I think we've talked enough."

"But you will not kill me now. You think you will take me to your Naples Control of K Section, yes? I am worth more alive than dead. You have had time to control anger and think about this. What I know would close many of your files back in Washington. So listen to my offer. Everything I do must end in profit. It is my first rule in life. Your death now will gain nothing for me. You are only a nuisance, an emotional indulgence, you and your pitiful little band of hoodlums. You are fond of Gabriella, but have you considered what tragedy you bring her to? Or have you considered that *she* might betray you?"

"Get to the point."

"I do so. I ask you to give up this foolish venture. O'Malley lied to you. He is a petty thief, and the Brothers must punish him, that is all. Zio cannot permit his breach of discipline. And since Gabriella associates with you, Zio condemns her, too." Karl Kronin hitched up his trouser leg an inch more. "So, yes, I get to the point. You will leave Naples tonight. You will fly back to the States. I give you back your life this way. And you will consider the problem entirely resolved."

Durell shook his head. "I think not."

Then the telephone rang.

The sound was discreet in the perfumed apartment. The instrument was at Kronin's elbow, and he looked at Durell as if for permission to answer it; but he did not wait for Durell's nod before he picked it up. His bald head shone glossily as he inclined his head to speak into the phone.

"*Pronto . . . Si, si . . . Sono qui . . .*" He listened and looked at Durell's tall, dark figure. His smile moved like a wound across his harsh face. He nodded again. "*Buono . . . Buono . . . Ciao.*"

He hung up and crossed his leg, careless of the gleaming metal that shone under his carefully creased trousers. "You lose, Cajun. Throw, game, and pot. Everything. You're *carnazza successe*—dead meat, as we say. That was a call from my men. O'Malley has come over to our side. We promised him amnesty for the little Gabriella, whom he loves so much. Such a weakness, love! O'Malley would do anything for our promise not to harm the girl. So now we have him and Gabriella."

"You're lying."

Kronin was not disturbed. "I never lie. You have nothing, I say. Like Dugalef, whom you killed, you no longer have even your life."

It was almost true.

It happened so fast that afterward Durell was unsure of what he'd seen. But he remembered thinking of Colonel Mignon's advice: *The man who wants to kill you had best do it himself.* He heard a click, and something moved in the shiny aluminum leg Kronin displayed. The sound, a brief *phut!,* came after he felt a stunning blow in his shoulder that knocked him back toward the balcony. *Too late,* he thought. *There wasn't anything in his dossier about gimmicks in his trick leg.*

He fired once, and again, but he was off-balance and not sure of his aim. Kronin moved with astonishing speed out of his armchair. At the same time, Durell glimpsed movement from the balcony, where a shadow abruptly blotted out the sunlight from the court beyond. He felt despair and a rage of defeat, and then something hit him and wiped out all the light completely.

HE SAID, "Ouch!" and he said, "Take it easy," and then he said, "I'm sorry about that."

"We all make mistakes."

"It was stupid."

"You couldn't know. Nobody knew."

"Turn off the light, will you?" he asked.

"The doc will be through in a minute."

"Is it bad?"

"You're lucky."

He could see nothing beyond the glare of the surgical light above his face. He hurt all over. He knew this couldn't be true and he concentrated on the pain and found that there was none in his left shoulder, only a feeling of something probing in there, and he guessed that was where the bullet went and where the surgeon was working.

"Kronin had a gun mechanism built into his metal leg," he said.

"That's right."

"How did *you* know?"

"You've been cursing it ever since we reached you in Adolfo's place, fifteen seconds after we heard the shot."

"Well, hell, where were you before that?"

"Listening. We had the place bugged in cooperation with the Naples *carabinieri.*"

"Are you a cop?"

"Cajun, don't you know who you're talking to?"

"No," he said.

"All right. In a minute. Doc, how is it?"

Another voice said, *"Sono finito."*

"Will I live?" Durell asked.

"Unfortunately."

"That's how I feel about it," Durell said.

"Here, swallow these pills."

"What are they?"

"Juice pellets. You'll be on your feet in half an hour. Riding high, wide, and handsome."

"Thanks, but I'd rather die." He swallowed the pills the hand gave him.

Onan McElroy was an elf in a green Borsalino, a silk suit, pointed Italian shoes, and an exclusive silk cravat from Theresa Barra's. He had big pink ears and a saddle nose and blue eyes as old and wise as a leprechaun's. His hair was the color of dirty sand. His brogue was atrocious, his Italian perfect, and he was the Naples resident for K Section. He smoked a crooked Italian cigar and fondled a bottle of Stravei, then poured it into a glass of red Campari and added a dollop of Beefeater gin.

"How," he said, and sighed with sybaritic luxury. "No bourbon?"

"At your elbow. Does the arm work?"

Durell tried it. "A little."

"It was a small slug, after all. It takes more than that to kill you."

"It knocked me down."

"Sorry, that was me coming in the window."

"What about Kronin?"

"Old Karl got clean away."

"How come?"

Onan McElroy said, "I told you, we all make mistakes. This was a day for it. Who killed precious Adolfo?"

"Kronin's people, I think."

"The cops want to know."

"Tell them anything," Durell said.

"Not good enough." McElroy pulled at one of his big pink ears. They sat in McElroy's small living room, where the doctor had patched Durell's wound. There was a view of the bay and the Amalfi peninsula creaming into the blue Mediterranean haze. Onan's cover for his job was as the owner of a fleet of Naples' notorious taxicabs. He was an Italian citizen, a bachelor of thirty-two, and in his spare time was an authority on the excavations at Herculaneum and an associate of the Naples National Museum. The books in his apartment proved it. When Durell looked at his watch and saw that it was just four o'clock, he was surprised. A lot had happened in a short time. Onan went on talking.

"The locals and Rome Interpol pegged Adolfo as their pigeon last month after the big hoo-hah about heroin refining here by the Fratelli della Notte. When were things different in Naples? But a few kids were caught when one died of an overdose, and the newspapers complained. Adolfo refined heroin as a sideline. I must say, I don't think the Fratelli worked that street so much. But trying to clean them out is like trying to clean up the Augean Stables, old Cajun." McElroy paused. "Adolfo was a weak flower, and the *carabinieri* had high hopes for him. Sooner or later they figured to nail him to the wall, screw him, and make him vomit all he knew, including dope on his precious aristocratic mother in her precious aristocratic palazzo on the Riviera de Chiaia."

"And now he's dead," Durell said.

"Now he's dead," Onan echoed, and downed his Stravei-Campari-gin mixture. "It needs some soda."

"Do the cops want me?"

"If they catch you, yes."

"Then I'd better move on." Durell stood up with care. "I'm worried. Kronin thought he had me in a box. He said O'Malley and the girl defected. I'd better go see."

"And if they have?"

"Then I'm up the creek."

"Do you want a lead, old Cajun?" McElroy grinned. "I've got a bypass out of that creek, but I don't know where it will take you. Ever hear of the Baron Uccelatti?"

"It's a familiar name. I'm worried about O'Malley and Gabriella."

"Well, they went thataway, partner."

"To Uccelatti? How do you know?"

113

"Private plane taxied right up the Castel dell' Ovo off the Partanope, near the rattrap apartment you took. Relax. You can't catch them this minute."

"Did they go willingly?"

"Who knows? They went. Laughing and smiling and the girl holding O'Malley's arm. One of my cabbies saw the whole thing. No visible guns in their backs."

"And the other two? Bruno and Joey?"

"Vanished. Lots of ratholes for rats in Naples, Cajun. Have some more bourbon. I'm not offering you my Stravei. It's hard to get. They don't export it to the States yet, either."

"What about Baron Uccelatti?"

"His plane. One of the richest men in Italy. Private yacht anchored at Palermo in Sicily right now. By air it's a short hop. They'll be landing in twenty minutes." McElroy consulted his Omega. His complicated model looked like an instrument off the panel of a seven-o-seven. "Yup, twenty minutes. But I don't advise you to follow."

"Why not? It's my job."

"They went willingly, Cajun. And you don't tangle with the *barone*. Next to Old Uncle he's top man in the hierarchy of the Fratelli della Notte."

"All the more reason," Durell said.

"You're out of your mind. You'll have to live on the pills, or your shoulder will cramp you more than a bit."

"I'll go now," Durell said. He stood up.

"Take your tux," McElroy advised. "Or I'll get one for you. Baron Uccelatti is a very high-living personality. Very formal. Like he's got a swarm of bikini girls all around him on that floating palace of a yacht. You'd look like a bum among them."

"I'll do the best I can," Durell said.

McElroy sighed and pulled again at his big ears. Durell wondered why they weren't longer.

"That's what I figured," McElroy said. He tossed Durell an Alitalia ticket envelope. "Your plane leaves in forty minutes for Palermo. I'll give you a supply of juice pills. Happy hunting."

HE BORROWED a book from Onan and read it on the plane to Palermo. The book dealt with castles and archeological sites on Sicily, and Durell searched it carefully for places that began with "San Gi—." He hoped Adolfo Cimadori's last words meant something. He hoped that Adolfo, out of his petty soul, had tried to spite his murderers by telling him where to find Vecchio Zio.

He found names such as San Giorgio and San Giuliano and San Gilo and San Giovanni and checked them against the sites marked on the folded map in the back of the book. They all seemed a long way from Palermo. And Palermo was where Gabriella began her trip fifteen years ago to visit Zio. It hadn't taken her too long, although she had slept in the car part of the way. Still, fifteen years ago Sicily had scarcely recovered from Operation Husky, and the roads were notoriously bad after the invasion chewed on them. She couldn't have gone more than twenty or thirty miles. But in which direction? He couldn't guess. He gave it up and took another of Onan's pills. His shoulder ached for a time and then the pain went away.

Long ago he had been intrigued by Sicily's eternal fascination, but he wished his return were under better auspices. The air at Boccadifalco Airport was immediately languorous, almost subversive with its soft appeal. It was dusk when he arrived, and the lights of Palermo around the Conca d'Oro were beads of pearls strung on the throat of the bay. Looming and brooding to the north like some ancient deity was the bulk of Monte Pellegrino, dominating this city of Carthaginians,

Greeks, Romans, Arabs, Norman conquerors, and that fantastic Swabian, Frederick II.

There was the usual crush and confusion at the airport, but he had no difficulty finding a taxi.

The taxi found him.

The man jumped out, saluted dramatically, and said, "At your service, signor. I am here through the compliments of Signor McElroy."

He was short and dark and looked like an Arab except for his blue Norman eyes. He was chewing a mandarin orange, and the taxi was redolent with the scent of citrus with a solid base of garlic.

"Why don't you announce it with a trumpet?" Durell objected. "Do you work for McElroy?"

"*Si*, signor. A great honor. This is his taxi. A branch of his business at Napoli. And my name, signor, is Michelangelo Cefalu."

"All right, Mike. I suppose you have a hotel all picked out for me?"

"Certainly. The Villa del Golfo, at Acquasanta. Very fine, very expensive. You are rich Americano, no?"

"No," Durell said. He was aware of Thompson's currency in his money belt. It would eventually present bookkeeping problems for K Section's accountants. "The room is reserved?"

"All is in order. Please to get in."

The trip was short, fast, and wild. An *A.Li.S.* helicopter beat the languid air overhead as they left the airport. He ate an orange out of a paper bag he found on the back seat of the taxi—after peeling it carefully.

The Villa del Golfo sprawled in its own park near the Piazza Acquasanta, a vast pile of architecture stamped with Palermo's unique history. The rooms held mosaic relics from surrounding ruins, and the windows were carved with Moorish filigrees. In the garden there were palm trees, oranges, and almond trees in flower, like a galaxy of earth-bound stars twinkling in the night. Durell was expected, although the hotel was filled with visitors to the local dog show and the restaurant jammed with tourists and proud Palmeritans.

His window faced the darkly glittering sea that had carried the galleys of Rome and Phoenicia and the ships of Aragon. There were tennis courts, and the parking lot was filled with a remuda of Mercedes, Ferarris and several Fleetwood Cadillacs. The orchestra in the dining room played "Gondolí, Gondolá," and sounded lonesome for Venice. Durell fanned the room for listening devices, then showered and ordered dinner sent up, a meal that included the Sicilian pasta *con sarde*, with a bottle of Faro wine. He began to feel lonely, too. The wine smelled of orange blossoms and bergamot. He took his glass out to the balcony and surveyed the beach and the waterfront.

There was a yacht basin not far off, and it was easy to spot Baron Uccelatti's *Vesper*. She was an auxiliary schooner of 110 feet, snow-white and floodlit, moored in wealthy exclusiveness some distance from the smaller boats that crowded the basin. The teak decks seemed aswarm with people, but it was too far off to make them out. Some were diving and swimming in the warm waters of the bay, tended by two small power boats that belonged to the *Vesper*. Most of the swimmers were girls, and most of what he could see of the girls was a lot of tanned and glorious skin.

He wondered how to manage a meeting with Baron Uccelatti. The informality aboard seemed promising, but it might also be an invitation to play Daniel in the lion's den. His shoulder began to ache again. The waterproof bandage was itchy. He flexed his left arm tentatively and tried to lift it with speed and accuracy, as if using a gun. The pain stabbed him, and he gave it up. He would have to fly on one wing. He owed something for this to Karl Kronin.

Then someone tapped discreetly on his door.

Presumably no one knew he was here but Onan McElroy. He asked who it was and heard the thick voice of Michelangelo Cefalu and opened it, using standard DUA procedure (Dangerous, Unknown Approach). It was just as well. The taxi driver was not alone. A tall man in a dinner jacket—he remembered McElroy's suggestion for his wardrobe—stood behind the Sicilian in a way that meant that Mike had a gun pointed at his back.

"I'm sorry, Signor Durell—"

"No matter. Who is your friend?"

"No friend, signor—"

The man in the dinner jacket spoke precise English. "I am sorry, too, sir, but it is necessary. We would not want you to refuse the baron's invitation."

"No, I wouldn't want to do that. What am I invited to?"

"He requests the pleasure of your company, sir," said the tall man. "Please do not disappoint him. He knows of you, you see. He looks forward to your visit to the *Vesper*."

Cefalu made pathetic, apologetic noises. So much for Onan McElroy's help.

"It's fine, Mike," Durell said. "You can go."

The formally dressed man nodded. When Cefalu scuttled away down the hotel corridor, Durell could not see a gun in the newcomer's hand. But it didn't necessarily mean there hadn't been one before. The man smiled pleasantly.

"I am authorized to tell you, sir, that you are given safe conduct and will be escorted back to the hotel before midnight."

"How much is the safe conduct worth?"

The other stiffened. "As much as Baron Uccelatti makes of it. He is a man of honor, if that relieves your fear."

"It would take more than that to relieve me," Durell said. "But nothing ventured, nothing gained, to coin a phrase. Lead on, my good man."

The man flushed, nodded, and waited for Durell to get his coat.

It was not a long walk to the yacht basin. The sea breeze was like a powder puff, and the scent of lemons made a counterpoint to the fading music from the Villa del Golfo. After a hundred yards they turned down a darker side street and came to an elaborate iron gate, which his escort opened with a touch of a finger on a small lion's head, and then they crossed a private garden lumpily shadowed with oleanders and palm trees. The lawn was like a Sarouk carpet. Ancient Roman statues loomed like shrouded ghosts in the gloom. Their feet made gritty noises as they walked along a shell path to the opposite gate.

Beyond the gate there was a glisten of water, a gleam of polished teak and brass, the lift and fall of a boat tender at a private dock. But they never reached it.

From the darkness beside the gate came quick leaping movements, a dull sound like the flat of a cleaver striking meat, a curse in Palmeritan accents. Inevitably Durell felt something slam into his wounded shoulder. The pain screamed down his arm, and he felt as if his fingers might drop off. His well-dressed guide made a small choking cry and went down and skinned his face on the oyster-shell path. He skidded a few feet and wouldn't need to shave for a while. Durell stepped to one side and leaned against a palm tree and watched two figures relieve the prone man of wallet, watch, gun, knife, small coins, cuff links, shirt studs, gold key chain, gold cigarette lighter, and gold cigarette case. There was a short grunting argument about the patent-leather shoes, and one of the shadows deftly removed them. Then he saw the glitter of a stiletto over the unconscious man's throat, and he pushed away from the palm trees, breathing thinly, and said, "Hold it, Mike."

Cefalu whirled. "Why? He would kill you!"

"I doubt it. And put back the loot."

"Have no doubts. They plan to kill you." Michelangelo Cefalu turned his dark face upward, perplexed. "Have you no gratitude?"

"He was taking me to Uccelatti, where I wanted to go. True, it wasn't on my terms. Put back the loot."

Cefalu said, "Two Fratelli wait on the dock. The water there is very deep. An accident, a stumble, a blow on the head and—poof! I have orders from Signor McElroy to protect you. Palermo is a wicked town, Signor Durell."

"Yes. Full of thieves. Don't kill him."

There was a quick argument between the taxi-driver and his friend. The second man settled for the shoes and trotted away. Cefalu dropped the oddments he had stolen back on the unconscious body, looked at Durell with sad solicitude, and clucked as he touched Durell's shoulder. "You are bleeding!"

"It's an old war wound. It bleeds when I'm frustrated."

"Come, we will attend to it. Not back to the hotel yet. They will look for you there. We will go to my place. There is much to be done tonight."

They walked out of the garden and back to the street the way they had come, turned down an alley, crossed a small piazza with a Norman church, went down another alley, and came to Mike's taxi. On the way Durell took two of Onan's pain-killers. In the cab Cefalu used a first-aid kit from under the front seat and deftly applied a fresh bandage to Durell's injured shoulder. Cefalu clucked again.

"What a nuisance. It inhibits you, eh?"

"I wish you hadn't interfered, Mike."

"What would you do? Go aboard and be slaughtered like a lamb? Demand that Uccelatti release the girl and turn her back to you? Pay ransom for her? No, no. The *barone* needs no money. He has everything and everyone you want, eh? Your friend O'Malley and the girl."

"And two other men. Brutelli and Joey Milan."

"No, he has no others. They escaped, I think. Guglielmo, my friend with the passion for shoes, saw it all. They jumped overboard, those two, and swam ashore before you arrived. There was a small regatta in process, you understand, and many people watching from the quays. It was impossible for Uccelatti to stop them." Cefalu paused. "Maybe we should find them first, eh?"

"It would help."

"And we will inquire about Gabriella Cimadori Vanini. A powerful name, a powerful family. You wish to find Zio, not so? You see, I am most logical. To find Vecchio Zio, you need the girl. But others in Palermo may remember her as a child and remember other things you must know. We will do both. We will look for O'Malley's friends and ask people about Gabriella."

Durell nodded. McElroy's pills were working.

A mile from Acquasanta's luxury hotels the city of Palermo properly began, curving around the harbor toward the dark loom of Monte Pellegrino. There are some areas in Palermo where no stranger in his right mind should walk alone. But Cefalu knew his city. They drove past the Foro Umberto and then up the Via Cerda, twisting and turning without prediction. Palermo was busy at this evening hour, which was still too early for dinner. Durell did not think they were followed, and Cefalu's evasive tactics took care of any chance of that. He decided that Cefalu might be right. Kronin had surely warned Uccelatti that he was coming. The Fratelli were both efficient and ruthless.

The dark streets canted steeply uphill at an angle that made the taxi shake and groan. Cefalu turned into another alley, came out on a tiny piazza where there was a magnificent view of the Opera House and the Cathedral, the latter like a fortress, even with its delicate Gothic towers. There was a glimpse of San Cataldo, with a bell tower that reflected Norman severity mixed with fanciful Arab grace, and red Byzantine domes squatting like enormous round eggs amid a nest of architectural tolerance. Then Cefalu plunged them back into another alley and halted before a singularly blank door.

"We will ask Mama Donatti first."

"Who is she?"

"A witch, perhaps. An old friend. She knows everything. She is a receiver of stolen goods." Cefalu rang the bell and shifted his weight impatiently. "Someone in this city must have useful information, signor. All we must do is find that certain someone."

A small girl with lank hair and a black dress that came down to her dirty ankles opened the door about two inches, listened to what Cefalu said in rapid

121

Italian, said, *"Si,"* and closed the door in their faces. They waited. The door did not open again. Cefalu knocked and pounded. No one came. Cefalu cursed. Then the little girl returned.

"Mama is not at home."

"Where is she, *carissima?*"

"I don't know."

"Can you let us in to wait for her?"

"It is not permitted. Mama does not wish to speak to you, signor."

"How do you know, if she is not at home?"

The child bit her lip and tried to slam the door shut. Cefalu would have smashed it open again, but Durell checked him. "Let it go. Try someone else."

They walked along twisting alleys between ancient tenements that were old when Frederick the Swabian ruled here in Byzantine magnificence, perhaps as old as the time when the Arabs flourished and sang their songs of praise to Palermo's beauty. Cefalu led them into a dark courtyard that smelled of things Durell did not care to identify, then up a moldy stairway to another door. Radios blarred. They heard the inanity of guitar-cum-folksong and a recording from Figaro. It made a curious antiphonal blend of sound. A stout woman in a black dress came to the door. She had been weeping. Inside, Durell glimpsed a wall of votary candles and an incredible display of icons, dominated by a plaster, painted statue of Santa Rosalia, the patroness of Palermo, who, although the daughter of a duke, died as a hermit in a cave on Monte Pellegrino.

"Cefalu, go away," the weeping woman said.

"But I must talk with you, Carmella."

"I have nothing to say."

"Are you afraid?"

"Am I stupid enough to be brave? Go away."

"You were told not to speak?"

"Yes, I was told."

"I have given you much business, Carmella."

"Not enough to buy my life."

"We look for two Americans. Two Fratelli."

"They are not Fratelli any more."

122

"But you know of them?"

"I cannot help you, Cefalu. You are a fool." She began to curse him without emotion and told him he was doing her great harm by coming to her. Cefalu gave it up and said, "We will try elsewhere."

On the way down the tenement stairs, Durell said, "It looks like the word is already out."

"Yes. They may not be alive any more."

They spent another hour inquiring among the warrens and hovels of Palermo. In some places the door was not even opened, although they could hear mutterings inside. In another, a man began to shout in a fine Sicilian rage and drew a knife on them. Cefalu retreated with many apologies. In a third place, a small bar, he went through the back doorway, curtained with stringed beads, and ordered wine from the thin, scuttling waitress. The wine never arrived. Two men who had been seated at a round, scarred table got up and left. After twenty seconds Durell suggested that they leave, too. Cefalu agreed it was a good idea.

"We will try some girls I know." Cefalu winked lasciviously. "My wife does not permit me to visit such terrible places, but after all, this is business."

The house was just around the corner from a red stone church with a facade of delicate Greek columns stolen from ancient ruins. The street was dark and cobbled. The house itself looked better than its slum neighbors. Durell suggested they try the back way in.

"No, no, that will be dangerous," Cefalu objected. "The bold, direct approach is always best here."

Cefalu insisted that this was their last hope. "I have brought many customers to Firenza's girls. It is a remarkable place. She owes me much. If anyone knows about Gabriella and your two friends, Firenza will have learned of it by this hour. And she will tell us."

A traditional red globe shone just inside the curtained doorway. The entrance was open. A man in a blue pinstriped suit, with black hair pomaded close to his narrow skull, jumped up and began to protest about something. Cefalu called loudly for Firenza, and there was a sudden break in the dance music they could hear from a parlor beyond, and a sudden babble of girlish voices, then a deep shout that should have been a man's but came from the madame's throat. Firenza swayed in, an enormously fat woman with a moustache, and flung her arms around the diminutive Cefalu in a greeting that crushed him against her bulbous breasts. She wore a lemon silk gown decked with fringes at the waist, and her face was a reflection of primitive joy.

"Michelangelo! Come in, come in!"

It was the first place they had been welcomed, and therefore Durell had to assume they had been expected and that it was a trap. He hoped the huge Firenza wouldn't hug him, with his aching shoulder. But the madame regarded him with an eye that weighed, measured, and evaluated his male attributes with an approving, professional eye. "Americano! You, too. Come in, and we have a party, yes?"

"We were just looking—"

"Then, look!" she said, and roared with laughter.

She urged them into the parlor. An elaborate Zenith hi-fi stereo player started up full blast next to a round bar positioned exactly in the middle of the room. The bartender had moustaches like Salvatore Dali. There were illuminated religious paintings on the wall, which was paneled with lemon silk that matched Madame Firenza's tasseled dress. Durell could see no windows. The barman's hands dropped out of sight, but Firenza spoke sharply to him, and the man shrugged and began mixing drinks again.

Aside from these two, and three self-conscious customers, well-dressed and prosperous, pretending to read newspapers, the room was filled with half-naked girls. They came in all shapes and sizes, to suit the varied tastes of Firenza's clientele, from a tall and lissome blonde in peekaboo panties to a short, stout, dark girl with an open kimono who stared at them with angry eyes and arms akimbo on fleshy hips. When they came in, the girls sprang to attention as if on command; they smiled, showed their teeth, rolled their buttocks, and strutted about the bar in postures both lewd and inviting. Someone turned the hi-fi up even louder when it played a tarantella. A few of the girls began to dance with each other, throwing back their heads and kicking off their satin slippers, letting out high, ululating cries, their bodies twisting orgiastically.

Durell felt a pair of somber brown eyes watching him, out of key with the mood of Firenza's house. This girl was different from the others. She looked American and wore a silver evening gown like the skin of a snake, designed to conceal nothing beneath it. Nevertheless, she had an air of detachment as she sat in a corner chair, ignoring the crudities of her playmates. She even wore a pair of studious Franklin reading glasses, and the book in her sleek lap was Voltaire's *Candide* in French. Her long hair was as silvery as her dress, but she couldn't have been more than twenty.

While he returned her stare Michelangelo Cefalu spoke urgently to Madame Firenza.

"We must talk in private, sweetheart," Cefalu told her. "It is very important."

"Oh, yes, so I have heard," Firenza said. "The city stinks of fear tonight, thanks to you and your tall friend."

"But can you help us?"

"Come with me. One cannot hear a thing over this stupid uproar. My private office, please."

They followed the stout woman down a pink-lighted hallway and through another door. The old-fashioned Victorian tassels and beads of the parlor yielded to a strictly modern business office that would have done credit to a Madison Avenue account executive's suite. There was a gleaming safe, steel filing cabinets, an address rack, a steel desk, comfortable chairs with orange foam-rubber cushions, and a long settee. The wall paintings were Dufys. The room seemed soundproofed. Mama Firenza squeezed her rolls of heavy fat into her desk chair and sighed, patted her curled hair, and touched the dark moustache over her wide mouth.

She had stopped smiling. She was not amused. "Cefalu—and you, Americano—you are both insane or idiots." When they said nothing, she added somberly, "And I am a fool to even allow you in here, to let it be known I speak to you, after all of Palermo was advised to shut its doors against you."

"Who advised it?" Durell asked in Italian.

"Speak English, please. I need the practice. It was the Fratelli della Notte, of course."

"Do they subsidize you?"

"Sponsor, let us say. I owe them much. They have been very good to me. I would not betray them, so it depends on how I can help you. Cefalu is my good friend. If I talk to you, it is only because I wish to get him out of this mess you have gotten him into."

Cefalu said, "It is a simple matter, *cara*. We look for two Americans, a Signor Brutelli, a Signor Milan—"

"I know, I know."

"Do you know where they are, dear?"

Madame Firenza fixed cold, shrewd eyes on Durell. "I understand you are very rich. I am told you have twenty-five thousand dollars to buy information."

"That's true," Durell admitted.

"You have this with you?"

"Perhaps."

"You do or you don't."

"I do."

"Buono. So I can find your friends. But you want more than that."

"We also look for Gabriella Vanini."

"She is with Uccelatti," she said promptly. "It is impossible to reach her."

"And the man known as O'Malley?"

"He is on the yacht, too. Not as prisoners. As guests. Will you pay me five thousand dollars? Now, in my hand."

"It depends on how you can help us."

"I am told that you really look for Vecchio Zio. This is true madness. One does not even mention his name. His power is great. Women pray to him as if to a saint. I cannot tell you where he is. I am reluctant to admit this, since you are rich and willing to part with so much

126

American money. But it is a fact of life. One does not talk about Zio."

"Long ago," Durell said, "when Signorina Vanini was a little girl, she was taken to visit Vecchio Zio. The journey started from Palermo. It cannot be far. Perhaps you can lead us to someone who also went on that journey fifteen years ago."

"I can," the woman said flatly. She put her jeweled hands on the desk, like two lumps of dough into which someone had spilled rubies and diamonds. "There was the driver of the car, and Contessa Cimadori, of course."

"The contessa will not help us."

"I understand." She looked sharply at Cefalu. "Are you sure you know what you do, Michelangelo? You cannot live in Palermo after this, I think."

"If we succeed," Durrell insisted, "we will all be forgiven."

"And if you are not, you are both dead men. . . . There was a driver and a nurse. They are both alive, both in Palermo. Quite nearby. But they have to be convinced." Two extrusions of the doughy thumb and forefinger, rolled together in the universal gesture for money. "Cash talks, eh?"

"Five thousand?"

"For them. Another five for me."

"It's a bargain."

"Done. You can pay me."

Durell reached under his shirt and unzipped his money belt and took out the Geneva currency and counted five thousand dollars. He placed it in Firenza's hands. The doughy fingers came alive, twisting and counting with marvelous rapidity. The woman's breathing sounded loudly in the modern office. Her huge breasts lifted like Etna in eruption. She had an obvious passion for money.

"And the other five?" she whispered.

"When you deliver the driver or the nurse."

"Done," she said again.

"How long will it take?"

"An hour. Make yourselves at home. Enjoy yourselves. Everything is on the house." She began to laugh uproariously, heaving and swaying and wiping tears from her powdered and rouged face.

Durell couldn't see anything that funny.

THE silver-haired girl with the Franklin half-glasses closed her Voltaire with a deliberate snap and walked across the room to Durell. It was difficult to see how she could maneuver that rich body in the skin-tight silver lamé dress. Every twitch of every muscle reflected provocatively as she came to him.

"Mr. Durell, you seem bored," she said.

She spoke American English. It was almost an hour later. The parlor of the establishment had been busy for a time, and most of the girls were upstairs with customers. The bartender with the Dali moustaches was counting his liquor supply. The hi-fi had been turned down to only a few decibels above the ear-splitting level. Durell had suggested that Cefalu stay with Madame Firenza while she pursued her quest and he returned to the reception room to stand guard against unexpected intruders. It seemed to Durell that Cefalu was taking far too much time.

"I'm not bored," he told the girl.

"This is a place," she said, "where time can be made to fly on wings of pleasure. This is where the best of all possible worlds can come true."

"For some men," he admitted.

"Yes. But you are not like most men." She took off her half-glasses. "My name is Lora Smith. I come from Kansas City. Isn't that a laugh?"

"I don't know. Is it funny?"

"Tragicomic. I've been studying you."

"And what have you concluded?"

"You're too good to waste, damn you. Did you know that Cagliostro, that fabulous man, came from Palermo?"

"No, I didn't know that. Thank you."

"So did Uccelatti. And Vecchio Zio."

"And?"

"You dope, they're going to kill you. Don't you know that, either?" She reached out a cool, slim hand. "Come with me."

"Where?"

"You can wait in my room. Or they'll do it right here, you poor fool. I saw it happen twice before. And my Ouija board tells me I should save you."

"When did you consult it?"

"Before you came. I believe in it. Don't laugh, or I'll smack you. I'm only trying to help."

"Why?"

"Because I like you. And I'm sick and tired, and bored to tears."

"They might decide to kill you, too, Lora."

"That wouldn't be any loss," she said, "except to a few of my very special, very rich, and very aristocratic customers who come sneaking in here to visit me."

"I think it would be a terrible loss," he said.

"Shut up. I know what you want and I could give it to you."

"For a price?"

"So I'm the whore with a heart of gold." She shrugged and smiled. Without her glasses her eyes were a brilliant brown, big and clear. "Yes, for a price. You only have a few more minutes. You'd better believe it."

"I do," he said. He stood up. "Let's go."

There was no chair in her room, and he had to sit on her chaste-looking tester bed. It was three flights up richly carpeted stairs to her quarters. Unlike what he imagined the other rooms in the crib might be, Lora Smith's bedroom looked like something out of an upper-middle-class Kansas City suburban house. There were white nylon swag curtains over the windows, a maple Colonial bedstead, a braided New England rug, a Seth Thomas nineteenth-century banjo clock. The walls were feminine pink, the dresser antique white. He was astonished and then decided that the virginal college-girl atmosphere probably appealed to the Palmeritan aristocrats who patronized her wares. It would titillate their cosmopolitan tastes.

"Oh, God," she sighed. She did something to her hair, and it fell in a silvery cascade about her shoulders. She picked up the white telephone. "It will take a little time."

She twisted her full hips as she stood beside the phone on the dresser, and a zipper began to run automatically down her back along a fine spine and an astonishingly slender waist. Her skin was a golden tan under the silver lamé. She talked into the phone in a rapid undertone too fast for Durell's rusty Italian to interpret. There seemed to be only monosyllables in reply. She spoke more urgently for a few more seconds, then hung up.

"They'll call back," she said.

"Who?"

"One of my friends."

"A business acquaintance?"

"Yes. A very rich and important man."

"Who?" he asked again.

"It doesn't matter. We must wait twenty minutes."

"I'm not so sure—"

"God, I've been lonely for a man like you." As she walked toward him the dress came all the way apart in two sections and fell in a soft slither of silver about her feet. She stepped out of it without a pause, with an expertise that impressed him. Her body was shockingly smooth and firm and strong as she pushed him back with a hand on his chest and fell upon him. Her mouth was avid, as if trying to devour him. He had the fleeting thought that she might be after the money in his belt, but her passion seemed valid enough.

"Please," she gasped. "Oh, please!"

Then she laughed, a small, deep, gurgling sound in her arched throat. She rolled across him, her body as smooth as warm, flowing water. "Darling. Oh, you poor darling." She reached for something under her virginal pillow.

Perhaps if her firm, golden hip hadn't pressed so hard

against his wounded shoulder as she wriggled and stretched over him, he would not have been warned. As it was, the spasm of pain was too much for the pain-killer pills in him. He lurched up with a small gasp, just in time to see her snake the knife out from under the silken pillow.

Lora made a thin hissing sound and plunged the knife at his chest. Her brown eyes were malevolent. She hated him, hated all men, and the gesture was an act of infinite retribution. The blade seemed to scream with light, as if flashed before his eyes, and he twitched aside, and it thudded into the soft coverlet. In an instant he rolled away from her, crouching on the bed as she came up on her knees and drove at him again. He parried with his right arm, caught the impact of her stroke against his wrist, and then swung with his left, heedless of the pain in his shoulder. She was good, quick as a lithe golden cat. He missed, lurched to one side, and the knife went hissing through his sleeve and plunged again into the mattress. He had time for only one more try. His fist made a hard, satisfactory sound as it made contact with her jaw. He did not hold any-thing back. She was knocked sidewise, her head and shoulders twisting as she slid off the opposite side of the bed, and she landed on the floor with a solid thump. Her flexed hips and sprawled legs still rested on the bed. She did not move.

Durell drew a long, shaken breath and pulled the stiletto from the mattress, broke the blade, and tossed it aside. He crawled on hands and knees across the bed and looked down her long naked body to her face on the floor beyond. Her eyes were closed. A trickle of blood came from a corner of her mouth.

"What for, Lora Smith?" he asked softly.

But he knew the answer already.

There was a back stairway from the third floor down to the main level behind the "reception room" and Madame Firenza's office. Durell moved quickly, closed the door to Lora's room, and walked in dark silence down the steps. There was no alarm. Radios played in various other rooms in the crib. He heard a girl cry out. A man spoke in a low voice. Another girl laughed. A glass broke behind still another door. But everything was quiet in the parlor when he returned.

The man with the Dali moustache was gone. The hi-fi stereo player was silent. Most of the lights had been put out except for an eerie blood-red trade lamp in the hallway. Not a girl was in sight.

"Cefalu!" he called.

There was no reply.

The door to Firenza's business office was slightly ajar. Durell flattened beside it against the wall. A hissing sound, like escaping steam, came from inside. It was someone's breathing. He went in quickly, using IPE technique, and came up from his crouch very slowly and carefully, his gun ready. Madame Firenza sat behind her modern polished desk as if she had never moved. The noises came from her. Her eyes were like marbles pushed by careless fingers into the dough of her face. They rolled toward him, then toward a corner of the sterile office. Flung like a rag doll into the corner was Michelangelo Cefalu.

His throat was cut from ear to ear.

"WHO?" he asked.

"I did it."

"Why?"

"He attacked me."

"*Attacked* you?"

There was more hissing of steam. It sounded as if
there was a leaky valve somewhere deep in that mountain of flesh garbed in the lemon silk dress. She laughed
and then coughed and sprayed thick gobbets of rasp-
berry drops over her pristine desk. The coughing went
on for a time, and then she raised a fat hand and
patted her mouth primly, like an old maiden aunt at
tea. Durell heeled the door shut behind him. There was
no window in this room, and he didn't like that. He
looked at Cefalu again. The taxi driver who had worked
for Onan McElroy was very dead. He had the thought
that Madame Firenza was dead, too, but she didn't
know it. The establishment of joy was rapidly turning
into a charnel house.

"Why?" he asked again.

She spoke carefully, bracing herself with both hands
on the desk. "I tried to do as you asked. Why not?
I am a free woman. I never feared a man in my life.
I made your telephone calls. The nurse who took
Gabriella to see Vecchio Zio is not in the city. She
has vanished. Perhaps gone to visit relatives in
Messina, they say. It is not true. They removed her."

" 'They?' "

"The Fratelli della Notte. There seems to be trouble
in the Brotherhood. There are always two sides to life,
Americano. The right hand and the left, the top and

the bottom, the light and the dark. There are two sides to the Fratelli, also, these days. It was difficult to choose. I made the wrong choice."

"I'd better call a doctor. Where did Cefalu get you?"

"It is deep inside. I have no pain. But a doctor will not help me. No doctor would dare come here now, even if it were of any use."

"Firenza—"

She laughed and coughed again and dabbed at the ruby drops on her mouth. "Did you think Cefalu was your friend?"

"He worked for a friend of mine. He was helping me tonight."

"You should think about it. When you are finished with me here, you should go to my kitchen in the cellar and eat and drink and think about it."

"I'm not hungry." He thought she had lost her wits. "Please go on, Firenza."

She spoke carefully. "The second call I made was to find the driver who took the child Gabriella to see Vecchio Zio many years ago. This call was more interesting than the first. I have connections, you see. Important men who are torn between fear of the Brothers of the Night and fear of what I can do to their reputations, because they have been clients of mine. It was not too difficult to learn the name of the man who drove Gabriella, long ago, to Vecchio Zio."

"And—?"

"I can still help you, Americano. Why not? Cefalu thought he was stronger than I. While I was talking on the telephone he came to me across the room and stabbed me. He thought I was finished. But my fat, which makes some men laugh and others desire me, saved me. I took the knife he had used, pulled it from my body, and cut his throat with it, as you see. And I am not sorry."

"You say you learned the name of the driver."

"Of course. He was—how do you say it?—a double agent. Working both sides of the street. It was Cefalu."

SHE DIED laughing.

It was quiet in the room and all through the house. Durell opened the office door. The hall was empty. He went away from the room with the bar and found the stairs to the cellar. A smell of cooking drifted up the narrow, whitewashed steps. The house was very old, and the stairs creaked as he went down. He had to duck his head under an old, blackened beam at the bottom of the narrow chute. Below, the kitchen was shiny and clean, with a red brick floor, an old-fashioned nickel-and-iron stove, a water pump handle above a wooden, zinc-lined sink, and strings of garlic, rosemary, basil, and tarragon hanging from hooks in the beamed ceiling, which also held netted hams and unidentified bags.

At the big stone, assiduously grinding herbs in a fine old brass mortar and pestle, was Bruno Brutelli. Seated at a table, immersed in a slick and glossy magazine with a photo cover of a racehorse, was Joey Milan.

Durell was beyond surprise.

Thin vermicelli was coming to a boil in a big enameled pot on the stove. The bubbling of water was accompanied by a thin, preoccupied whistling from between Joey Milan's teeth. Bruno heard him first, turned his huge body, and looked at Durell from under beetling brows. His eyes were calm.

"Hey, Joey, he's here. Just like she said."

"What happened to you?" Durell asked quietly.

"We faked out," Milan said. "We didn't like the scene on Uccelatti's yacht."

"They just let you go?"

136

"Well, not exactly."

"Are they looking for you?"

"Sure, but some friends of Bruno's, relatives here in the old country, sent us here. You know how Bruno is. He likes kitchens. We been waiting an hour for you. The madame said you'd be down."

"What about O'Malley?"

They looked at each other. Bruno made a disparaging sound. Joey Milan began to whistle again.

"They still got him," Bruno grumbled.

"He didn't want to come with us," Joey said.

"And Gabriella?"

Both men shrugged.

"Is she on the *Vesper*?"

"We didn't see her." Joey Milan put away his shiny racing magazine. "We talked it over, Bruno and me, and we figured Frankie put his money on the wrong horse."

"Who are you betting on now?" Durell asked.

"You, Cajun."

"All the way?"

"Win, place, and show."

"Then, let's go," Durell said.

Bruno protested. "We've got time. You can't get herbs like these back in the States. Or this pasta. I never finished the vermicelli *a la putana* in Naples." His ugly face grinned. "I figure this is the right place to cook it. It don't take the girls long between tricks."

"If we stay here much longer," Durell said, "it will be your last meal."

They walked together through the dark alleys of Palermo's slums toward the bright center of the city. It was ten o'clock. The evening was soft and languorous, redolent with the scent of orange blossoms. The almond trees in the piazzas twinkled with white and pink flowers. Beyond the Piazza della Vittoria they passed the Sclafani and Royal Palaces, built by the Arabs for their emir and later Normanized and rebuilt for Frederick II's seat of government. They turned right beyond the cathedral, which had been founded by an English priest

137

named Walter of the Mill. The Palmeritans remembered him as Gualtiero Offamilio. At the Quatro Canto they turned left down the Via Maquedo. Durell felt better in the crowds of strollers and traffic.

On the way he explained what he wanted to do. Both men were dubious, but he led them back along the waterfront toward Acquasanta and the Villa del Golfo. An Alitalia jet to Naples shook the stars overhead. There was a constant uproar from motorboats and water-skiers off the beaches, a counterpoint of music from the sidewalk cafes, a hum of traffic along the boulevard.

"It's crazy," said Joey Milan.

"There's nothing else to do," Durell told him.

"We could always go home."

"You'll never leave Sicily alive unless Old Uncle lets you."

"So who will talk to us?" Milan asked.

"Maybe Uccelatti."

Both were silent except for a small growl of disbelief from Bruno. Durell turned onto a public dock, where signs advertised boats for hire. They were near the yacht basin, and he could see the lights of *Vesper*, moored in splendid solitude apart from the other yachts. The wash of a passing water-skier splashed under the dock, and they were besieged by boatmen arguing the virtues of their craft.

"Do we just ride up there?" Milan asked.

"Why not? He wanted to see me earlier."

"Well, he don't want to see *us*. We left without sayin' good night."

"It will be all right," Durell said. He wished he felt as confident as he sounded.

They approached the schooner from the darker sea side, although floodlights on the tall masts played on the water around the white hull for the swimmers who sported there. Durell saw several mess-jacketed crewmen hustling drinks for the girls who sprawled like golden nymphs on deck, or who occasionally dived overboard for a brief swim. The girls far outnumbered the men. Someone had a movie camera aboard, and

138

there was much shouting and directing and laughter mingled with obscene insults.

"They make a film," said the boatman. "The sainted *barone* is a patron of the arts, *si*? He is much involved with starting a motion picture industry in Sicily to rival that of Rome. It will be a success. Whatever he does, it will be a success."

"I don't see the baron aboard," Durell said.

"Oh, he is there. Probably below, talking business." The boatman looked doubtfully at Durell. "You are sure you are invited to *Vesper*? If not, I will stand by to fish you out of the sea when they throw you off, eh?"

There was a small landing stage to port. One of the attendants hurried to the polished rail, saw Durell, and vanished. A girl scrambled up on the landing, shook her wet blonde hair and her body, which was scantily covered with a mesh suit of only about four square inches of solid material where it counted. She splashed water at Durell and laughed and ran up the ladder. He thought briefly of Lora Smith, out of her silver lamé gown, on her back with her legs up on the bed. He felt a momentary regret. Then he followed her aboard.

He did not see O'Malley. The moton picture work went on forward, detached from the rest of the activity. Then the same man who had originally picked him up at the hotel walked aft, eyebrows lifted in surprise.

"Signor Durell, you are welcome." He wore a fresh white dinner jacket and a piece of Band-Aid on his handsome aquiline face. "I am Pietro. We never introduced ourselves." He peered over the side at Bruno and Joey. "You have lost Cefalu, your impetuous friend?"

"Yes, you might say that."

"Good. Then come with me, please."

"One moment. Is O'Malley aboard?"

"Baron Uccelatti will explain everything."

They picked their way across golden legs and rounded thighs and trays of drinks on the teak deck.

Pietro looked sidewise at him and licked his lips and then opened a cabin door that led down into the main salon.

"Up forward, *per favore*."

"You first," Durell said.

The man smiled sadly. "You forget, it was I who was taken by surprise the last time."

There were rich and simple furnishings, mahogany paneling, a polished chart table, shining brass clocks and barometers, tangerine-colored settees and chairs, and watered silk curtains over the big portholes. Durell followed the tall man down three more steel-plated steps into a stateroom corridor. The cabin he entered was fitted out as a combination sitting room and study. The man behind the kidney-shaped desk arose graciously as he came in and walked forward with an extended hand.

"Mr. Durell, welcome. I had grave fears for your safety when Pietro came back alone and told me how you had been intercepted. I am Uccelatti."

They shook hands. Uccelatti was an urbane Italian whose smiling confidence reflected wealth, perfect grooming, and a cultivated sensibility. His English was only faintly accented. He had thick, peppery hair, a smoothly shaven olive face, and diamond-brilliant blue eyes. His teeth were white and even. He waved his hand graciously for Durell to be seated.

"Bourbon is your drink, is it not?"

"Thank you. But I don't intend to be your guest for long, invited or not."

"But you *are* invited, my dear sir. Did I not send Pietro for you? On my honor, I have been most anxious to meet you. You have my word that we are not enemies."

"That remains to be seen."

Uccelatti wore a silk ascot the color of Marsala wine, with fawn-colored slacks and chalk-white sneakers. His grip was slightly callused, as a seaman's should be. He dismissed Pietro with a nod. It was quiet in the cabin except for the muffled noises from the bikini girls on deck.

"You must excuse the external impression the

140

Vesper must give you. It is amusing to have these people aboard. And the young ladies are decorative, eh? You must realize I deeply regret this entire affair, and I wish with all my heart that it had not occurred. I am glad you arrived here safely. Your position in this business is quite well known to me. We have an adequate information service, of course. It is necessary, for one to survive."

"You do very well," Durell said.

Uccelatti smiled. "I was born to accept the responsibilities of wealth along with the honor of my name. A noble title means little today, but it is an anachronism to which I cling out of sentiment and because here in Sicily the people prefer the old ways. It gives them a comforting sense of continuity. Our worlds are not the same, Mister Durell, and I grant that mine may be only a fading dream. What I possess must be paid for, and I do so daily." The baron waved a mild hand. "But you did not come here to listen to idle and perhaps useless conversation."

"You know why I am here," Durell said.

"Indeed. And you bring me risks that I could easily avoid by refusing you a single word."

"I want the girl, Gabriella Vanini—and I want my friend O'Malley released. Is he aboard?"

"He came of his own free will, sir."

"Is he also free to leave?"

"No," Uccelatti said. "I am sorry."

"And Gabriella?"

"Do nothing rash, Mister Durell, until we have exchanged views, I pray you. You are angry and suspicious. But I am, too—more than you. When you are finished in Sicily, you will go about your business elsewhere in the world. But I must go on living here, if possible, and try to survive."

"What are you afraid of?" Durell asked.

"More accurately, I am concerned—very deeply— for what is happening. I sense contempt in your attitude. You think of me as a criminal, battening on sin and vice. It is not so. I accept nothing for myself from the Fratelli."

141

"You don't deny membership in the Brotherhood?"

"I deny nothing because I need your help. I am perplexed, and you may be the only man to solve my problems. So we meet like this. Let us not behave like two jungle animals who meet on the same trail after the same prey. But perhaps I can explain more clearly if I tell you why I named my yacht the *Vesper*."

Durell moved a chair against the bulkhead and sat down. The cabin was warm, although the ports were open and a faint sea breeze stirred the silk curtains. Dimly he heard cries from the girl swimmers, a shout from the cameraman, and a little thud on the deck overhead.

"Our history has been long," Uccelatti said, "and ancient and troubled. Of the original Siculi, none lived after the Greeks came to Syracuse. Our island has always been used by conquerors, from the Greeks to the Arabs and the Normans. Sicily has been a rich hunting ground for such predators. And the people received nothing but slavery and feudal oppression from those who came to 'liberate' us. We were misruled by the ancient Carthaginians and the Bourbons. We are now Italian but not of Italy. There were once giants in our land, remembered by the villagers, who carry figures of these legendary Giganti in their annual processions. We dwell among roses and almond blossoms, but their scent does not cover the stink of oppression that led Sicilians to rebel time and again against rich landlords and foreign nobles, thieves of our natural wealth. Long ago there was an insurrection against the House of Anjou, which succeeded the court of the Swabian, Frederick the Second. For six centuries, from twelve eighty-two, Sicilians were crushed between dishonest rulers from Anjou, Spanish viceroys from Aragon, and Austrian legates. That rebellion in twelve eighty-two was led by men who called themselves Vespers, Mr. Durell. I have remembered them in the name of this vessel. For six hundred years after that revolt the Sicilians hatched plots, planned executions, fought in the villages and the hills—and were always crushed. The survivors inevitably fled into a life of desperate outlawry." Uccelatti smiled thinly. "The life of a bandit was at least free, you see. And it became the habit of our island."

"The Mafia?"

"And others. Robin Hoods sometimes, murderers and thieves at others. I make no apologies or excuses. It was a necessity. It was war."

"It's not the same today," Durrell said. "The Black Hand, the Cosa Nostra—"

"We are the Fratelli della Notte."

"Is there a difference?"

"Until recently, yes. True, we lived on crime. But it was neither violent nor vicious. And our charities—"

"And murders—"

"These are only late developments."

"This is the source of your distress?"

"Yes, it is." A thin shine of sweat showed on the baron's fine face. "I am more than distressed. I admit I am desperate."

"Did the change come," Durrell asked quietly, "when Kronin entered your organization?"

"That filth," Uccelatti said.

"Isn't he your superior now?"

"He thinks so."

"Where is he now, by the way?"

"As far as I know, he is still in Naples."

"Dollars to doughnuts he's close by."

"No, I would know of it."

"You don't know anything." Durell spoke angrily. "You've been tricked and betrayed. It was nice to hear your little historical lecture, but it only proves you do live in an unreal world of romantic nostalgia for the past. It's suicidal. The world has changed, and if you don't change with it, you are doomed."

The baron bowed his head. "I know all this."

"But what are you doing about it?"

"I do not know what to do."

"Well, for a start, you can tell the truth about Kronin, Zio, and Gabriella. Tell me how Kronin took over the Fratelli to use them to establish a sabotage net in my country, like cancer cells in my nation's bloodstream."

"You are angry, Mr. Durell."

"It might help if you were angry, too. How did Kronin get into the Fratelli della Notte?"

"Vecchio Zio ordered it. He is our chief. One gives him unquestioned obedience."

"He may be senile, a very old man."

"Yes he is old."

"Is he actually alive?"

"Yes."

"Have you seen him lately with your own eyes?"

There was a moment's hesitation. "Yes."

Durell said, "You're a liar, Baron."

Uccelatti flushed. His hands trembled. A motorboat went by, and the wake rocked the schooner slightly. "I saw him, but it was under peculiar circumstances. I am not sure—" He paused.

"Not sure of what?" Durell asked.

"Karl Kronin stood beside him. Almost prompting him, I thought." Uccelatti sighed. "I grew suspicious then. But one does not lightly disobey Zio. The orders are explicit. I must obey. It is the rule. Without obedience we die."

"Where do you fit into the hierarchy?"

"Until Kronin appeared, I was Zio's right hand. But now—I am nothing."

"And you don't like it," Durell suggested.

"They wanted to kill Gabriella."

"They certainly tried," Durell said grimly. "If she's still alive, let me see her."

"I am sorry, she is not aboard."

"Then, where is she?"

"I could not believe Zio ordered her death. It came from Kronin. Knowing this, I sent Pietro to Naples, to O'Malley. I promised him safety for himself and Gabriella. O'Malley was angry and jealous of you, in any case. And I had to learn the truth. I do not know it all yet, but soon I shall. I must. So I took matters into my own hands."

"What have you done?"

"I sent Gabriella," said Uccelatti, "to Vecchio Zio."

144

DURELL let out a long, slow breath. It was as if a tightly coiled spring inside him had relaxed a bit now. The baron clenched his trembling fingers. The sweat stood out in great beads on his handsome face; his blue eyes were dulled now. There was a knock on the door, and Uccelatti said, "Come in," and Pietro entered.

"What is it, Pietro?"

The man looked at Durell. "Your friends want to come aboard to see if you are safe. I told them to wait, but it is difficult to tell them anything."

Durell stood up. "One more thing, Uccelatti. You understand that you may have sent Gabriella to her death?"

"I know this."

"How long ago did she leave?"

"It has been over three hours. But it takes perhaps two to reach the place."

"Where is it? And how many men went with her?"

The baron looked desperate. "None." He looked at Pietro. "I considered it safest to send her alone. Whom could I trust as a guard? You have described my situation very exactly, Mr. Durell. I am betrayed, lied to, and I know no man I could trust to keep her alive."

Durell looked at Pietro. "What about him?"

"Not even Pietro."

The other man's face was like stone.

"You've probably killed her," Durell said.

"No, there is a family in the hills—peasants, or at least they live like peasants. An old man and a woman. They live near her destination. I told her to go to them before she finished her journey."

"And can you trust them?"

"Why not? They are my father and mother." Uccelatti shook his troubled head. "You must understand more, Mr. Durell. Although I carry a noble title and had dreams as a boy far beyond our means, I did not always live like this. The war and the Mussolini years did strange things to everyone. I was born in Sicilian poverty—a very special thing. It is hopeless, but not degrading. One survives somehow—and the Fratelli helped us. My parents were caretakers for Vecchio Zio. He took an interest in me and started me on the upward path, educated me and gave me all I needed to assume my hereditary place. I was foolish, vain, ambitious. In return I did all he asked. Eventually I was set up with the *Vesper* and became a 'respectable' businessman, an industrialist. And, of course, all the Fratelli funds were channeled through my organizations. They still are. It is the price I paid."

"And now you regret it?"

"No, I only regret Kronin. He came into the picture through me. As a boy, I was filled with revolutionary fire. The people were oppressed, savagely mistreated. I sought for years to help them, through youthful idealism. I joined the Communists. Does that surprise you? I am still a member. That surprises *me,* you see. And not long ago, when I was at Dubrovnik, in Yugoslavia, ostensibly on a pleasure cruise, I was ordered to report to Albania."

"Then, you tried to serve two masters."

"Yes. A stupid donkey straddling a deep stream. In Albania I met many Chinese Reds from Peiping. I was treated with much respect. They knew all about me. They had been holding me as a silent agent until a time when I might be useful. Their hatred for your country, Mr. Durell, goes beyond all reason. They decided that the time had come to use me and use my position in the Fratelli della Notte."

"That's where Karl Kronin came in?"

"I was ordered to recommend him to Vecchio Zio for his present position. I obeyed. It was that or my destruction. They knew all about my false business enterprises, enough to put me in jail for life as a criminal.

I had no choice. And at first I saw no real harm."

"And Zio accepted Kronin?"

"Yes."

"Knowing who and what he is?"

"I am not sure about that. I was not admitted to their councils after the first meeting. When I went to Zio recently, I was told nothing and ordered to keep silent. Zio gave me these orders." Uccelatti stood up. "My life is in the balance now. I am a rebel, you might say. By talking to you, I forfeit everything, according to the Fratelli law. But the time has come for decision. Either I am a fool and so deserve to die, or a great evil has been done, which only I can correct. So I have told you everything."

"Not everything," Durell said.

"What more can I do?"

"Two things. I want O'Malley first."

"I cannot release him."

Durell was impatient to be moving. Every moment counted, and he felt time slipping inexorably away. "What you want O'Malley for," he said flatly, "is as a hostage to fortune in case you've made a mistake. But you can't have it both ways. You must commit yourself or you're a dead man, Uccelatti. You know this, but you don't want to face it. But you've come too far to my side now. Keeping O'Malley for Zio's revenge later won't help."

Uccelatti was a tormented man. The sound of sprightly music on deck sharply contrasted with his haunted eyes as he looked at Durell's implacable figure. He shuddered violently, then was still and regarded Pietro. "What do you think, my friend?"

Pietro seemed shocked at this request for his opinion. "I do not know, *Barone*. He sounds logical."

"We are emotional, not a logical people. It is a bad fault." He turned to Durell again. "You asked for two things. O'Malley first. Very well, you can have him. And the second matter?"

"Tell me where to find Vecchio Zio. You sent Gabriella there, and Kronin will kill her. I don't know about this old wizard godfather of hers. That's what I must find out. There is a mystery here, and it must be resolved if any of us are to stay alive. So tell me the way. Now is not the time to stick to the rules."

Uccelatti said, "But if you try to get in by force, you will never make it alive. Believe me. There are traps. That place is impregnable. Much as I respect your ability, Signor Durell, you will find it too much even for your talents. It is the best-kept secret of the Fratelli. Zio is our chief. He has led us for two generations. He is almost a myth today except to a few of us. One does not even mention his name lightly, as you do."

"You must tell me," Durell said.

Again the man sighed, then straightened and stood up. "Pietro, release O'Malley. See that he has some food and wine. Quickly! As for you, Signor Durell, I fear I send you to your death. But you insist, and I will not deny you. We are lost in any case. That poor girl, that poor Gabriella—"

"What is the name of the place?"

"It is in the mountains. It is called Sangieri. It is an old stronghold, not well known to historians. It is not easy to find. I will describe to you the roads you must follow and I will give you a car to go there."

O'MALLEY said, "It's past midnight. You sure this is the right way?" He rubbed his wrists, where he had been bound helplessly in the *Vesper*'s engine room.

They had followed Route 186 southwest out of Palermo, climbing the hills to Monreale. Beyond the royal pleasure grounds of ancient Norman kings they drove by the wine-colored cathedral with its Moorish cloisters. Only an occasional truck or flashy sports car passed them toward the city. Uccelatti had lent them his gunmetal Jaguar with its built-in bar and two-way radio. The night cooled rapidly as they followed the twisting road into the spiny hills. Durell drove. From Monreale they cut left along a secondary road, picked up the larger highway 586 to Altofione, then climbed again along a twisting route out of the valley toward Lago di Piana d'Albanesi.

O'Malley sat beside Durell on the front bucket seat. Bruno and Joey sat in the back. There was an air of constraint among all of them. A few minutes after O'Malley spoke Durell found the small graveled road that ran south across a small bridge and then wound into the barren, treeless mountains of interior Sicily.

"You waiting for an apology, Cajun?" O'Malley asked finally.

"You don't owe me anything," Durell said.

O'Malley looked wolfish in the glow from the walnut-veneered dashboard. "I figured the odds at seven to five I made the right break."

"You gambled with Gabriella's life when you pulled out in Naples."

"I figured it was helping her, Cajun. And the way

149

she looked at you and depended on you." O'Malley paused. "So I was wrong. I was stupid. I never wanted to put her in danger by goin' to her. She comes first with me. When I saw what happened, I decided to hell with patriotism and I tried to pull her out of it the best I could. So thanks for getting me out of the jam—after I was so dumb about it."

"We're not out of it yet. Gabriella's had a long start. Kronin might have her by now."

"Don't rub in the salt, Cajun."

"You need it," Durell said.

The lush coastal area of palms and almond trees was far behind. The mountains, long stripped of their forests by ancient seafarers for ship timbers, looked barren and desolate. Now and then they passed a shepherd's hut, dark and forlorn, in the craggy defiles. The air turned chilly. There were no road signs. Now and then a rutted trail led from the road Durell followed, and once he lost a precious five minutes at a fork where the branches seemed equally important. Low stone walls lined their way.

"Are we getting anywhere?" O'Malley asked.

"I'm just following directions," Durell said.

"That Uccelatti is scared out of his skin. I wouldn't trust him. He promised he'd take care of Gabriella, then he clobbered me and tied me up and sent her off into this crazy country all alone to see this great-grand-uncle of hers. Sending an innocent girl to do his dirty work! Like sending a child on a truce mission to the Vietcong. They'll zap her on sight."

O'Malley's yellow eyes were savage in his narrow hunter's face. Durell sensed a change in him. Desperation was the main evidence. He remembered O'Malley as a laughing, reckless boy; but he was different now. It was a quality of doom that Durell had seen in other men, a sense that life was of no further importance. He began to wonder if it would not have been better to leave O'Malley on the *Vesper*.

They were all armed, but there was no guessing their needs when they arrived. Uccelatti could give no details of the headquarter's defenses. And somehow Durell was sure that Karl Kronin was there waiting for them. It could be a trap. But he had to walk into it.

They roared through another dark village with blue Arab doors—the blue symbolized the gates of heaven—and the houses were dark and shuttered against the full moon as it shone on the bleak poverty of these mountains. The inevitable cathedral soared with ironic, airy grace, like a Moorish dream, into the pale night sky. Then the rutted road led them up a narrow valley, hemmed in by craggy heights, where a small stream rushed southward in silvery froth. They turned left again. The stone walls that protected them against the dizzy drops gradually eroded, and the stiff springs of the Jaguar jounced heavily. Durell gripped the wheel hard to keep them on the path.

They ended abruptly in a stony pasture. He braked the car. The powerful engine ticked over, purring like a sleepy cat. They should be near their destination now, but there were no signposts to indicate a place named Sangieri. The moonlight mocked him. The stars laughed. The mountains sang of their silence.

"We're nowhere," O'Malley sighed.

"Lost?" Bruno rumbled.

"That son-of-a-bitch-Uccelatti," O'Malley said. "I'll kill him if anything's happened to Gabriella."

Two goats grazed within the bounds of the stony field. There was no sign of a house. He slammed the Jaguar into reverse and roared back for perhaps a hundred yards. He had missed the tracks that curved to the left in the straggly grass. He started the car that way.

"This ain't no road," Bruno objected.

"There's been a car ahead of us," Durell insisted. "You can see the tire marks in the grass."

"Like I don't see nothing," Bruno grunted; but he subsided and clung to the strap as they bounced over stones and ruts that seemed to lead nowhere.

Durell used only the dimmers as they crawled ahead. He was looking for the cottage where Uccelatti said his parents lived. If Gabriella came this way, there had to be a sign soon. His sense of lost time grew more acute.

The Jaguar stalled. He started it again, regretting the engine noise. The dim path led along a grassy ridge that bordered a sheer drop into a rocky valley. The road twisted south, and it seemed as if they had lost all contact with civilization. He was not even sure he could see the trail of the other car now, and he wondered if his imagination had played a trick on him.

"Hold it," O'Malley said.

Durell looked at him and saw a gun in O'Malley's hand. The man's eyes gleamed with an angry, feral light.

"What is it?"

"I thought I heard somebody yell. Like a scream."

"Man or woman?"

"Gabriella."

Durell urged the big Jaguar forward again over a wilderness of bumps and rocks. Abruptly the way sloped down into a cuplike depression, where cedar trees screened them from the surrounding mountains. He listened for anything O'Malley might have heard above the low hum of the engine; but he heard nothing.

"There," O'Malley said.

His word came like a small explosion, and he pointed to a rough stone wall that barred their way. There was a wooden gate, and beyond it was a well-defined path. The gate stood open, like an ominous invitation for them to enter. Durell drove through.

The heavy car responded gratefully to the solid road-bed. The trees lined each side of the route, cutting off their view. Certainly no wandering tourists could ever find this place beyond the pasture where the goats were tethered. Then a rocky bluff barred their way. The road vanished through a small hand-hewn tunnel. On the other side, when they came out, they saw the house.

It was of stone, small and neat, with a red tiled roof that looked black in the moonlight, and a square tower at one end. A low wall enclosed a garden plot and a few fruit trees that lifted twisted arms to the inhospitable environment. The wooden shutters looked tightly shut on all the windows; but Sicilians were adverse to the night air and the dangers of banditry. Yet the front door, a massive affair with metal straps, stood ajar.

Durell checked the car, switched off the engine, and listened. All he heard was the singing of the mountains. The bonnet gave off a soft metallic *ping!* as the cool wind struck its heat. O'Malley gave a great start.

"Take it easy," Durell told him.

"I don't see no headquarters pad around here."

The house was much too small for what they sought. But it could be where Uccelatti's parents lived. Beyond the house was a rise of ground and a row of cypress trees. The road went around the house, but he could not see how much farther it proceeded.

"Bruno. Joey," Durell said. "Get to the fence by the garden and watch that front door. Don't go in the house. O'Malley and I will case the back. Wait until you hear from us before you move. And don't shoot at anything until you're sure of what it is. Let's go, Frank."

O'Malley slid out with quick and silent grace. The night wind slapped them with chilly force. The pasture offered no cover as they circled the dark and silent house. They went through the cypress grove, and Durell pointed to the tire marks of cars.

"More than one," he said softly.

O'Malley's face was lumpy with corded muscles along the jaw. His blond hair blew in the wind. "Cajun, if anything happens—"

"Plenty is going to happen."

"I mean, to me. Or to Gabriella. I want you to know why I creamed out in Naples. It wasn't the money they offered. Or the immunity. It was Gabriella. The way she looked at you and began to depend on you. I got stupid about it. She doesn't know about men. She's the most innocent girl I ever met. She's got a—a beautiful soul." O'Malley spoke between clenched teeth. Durell started forward, and again O'Malley checked him. "Listen, Cajun. The way she looked at you—well, she worships the ground you walk on, you know that? She's vulnerable. I never could get her to look at me like that."

"I didn't encourage her," Durrell said. "And she loves you, Frank."

"I'm not so sure. But all of a sudden it doesn't mat-

153

ter so much. I mean, about me and her. I'm only worried about Gabriella. Cajun, they'll *kill* her!"

"Yes," Durell said.

"I just want you to know I'm not sore now about how she feels about you."

"You're wrong about that. But there is her car."

He pointed to a small Fiat parked in the dooryard behind the stone house. There was still no sign of life about the place. More goats were tethered in the yard, and one of them bleated softly and stamped small hooves as they approached. It was a giveaway that could not be avoided, but Durell swore softly. In a low shed with one side open to the south he made out an elaborately decorated Sicilian farm cart, the bulk of a draft horse in a stall, and the glimmer of pitchforks and farm tools. A haycock stood to the left of the shed.

A small, slight figure stood just to one side of the haycock, crying softly in the night.

It was Gabriella.

SHE LOOKED at them with wonder as they came near and she swallowed a last sob and gave a small cry of gladness and ran toward them. O'Malley stiffened as her arms came up, outstretched. Then she flung herself at him.

"Frank! Oh, Frank!"

Durell saw O'Malley look at him over the girl's head. His face reflected remorse and relief. O'Malley kissed her, murmuring, and stroked her long hair, while Durell turned and considered the dark farmhouse and the surrounding grounds. He saw no danger anywhere.

"Cajun?" Gabriella whispered.

Her face shone with tears. She rubbed them away with the back of her hand, a child's gesture. "Oh, I'm so glad you're here. I thought you'd never come."

Durell looked at O'Malley. "Satisfied now?"

"Like I apologize, Cajun."

Durell turned to the girl. "What happened here?"

"Those poor people the Uccelatti's—are in the house, so beaten—"

"Still alive?"

"Y-yes, but—"

"No one else around?"

"I saw no one. But it must have happened just before I got here. They knew I was coming." She turned. "O'Malley, there is terrible danger here. I hid in the shed for a time and then I heard a car and I waited, ready to run. But then I saw you and somehow—it was stupid of me—all I could do was stand here and cry."

"Do you remember this place now?" Durell asked.

"Yes, it has all come back to me. The Fratelli head-quarters is just over that rise." She pointed. "But it is impossible—" She paused again, then smiled with wet, tear-stained lips. "No, nothing is impossible to you and O'Malley." She kissed Durell briefly. Her face was salty against his mouth. He turned her gently back to O'Malley and said, "Let's go see the old people."

The house was clean, whitewashed, furnished with heavy Spanish chairs and tables, brass and copper cookware in the kitchen, thick rugs, ornately carved wood, and a coat-of-arms plaque over the stone fire-place. Footsteps scraped painfully toward them in the moonlit shadows, and a tall old man with white hair, stained with blood, appeared.

"Gabriella, child?"

"It is all right, *barone*. These are the American friends I told you about. How is the signora?"

"I have attended to her." The man's face was bruised, and he walked stiffly, but still with pride and defiance. "Do not concern yourselves with us. We are old, but we shall survive. Only Zio is important now." He turned to Durell. "I have not been permitted to see Zio for a month. No one knows what is happening over there. We wrote to our son and asked for his help. It was a hard thing to do, for I never approved of the way he shaped his life. My years are too many to change my ways, and my wife and I have been satis-fied in this rustic place. But it must be different for Gabriella. You must help her. And her only hope is to bring her face to face with Zio and ask his forgiveness."

"But I have done nothing wrong, *barone*."

"Then, you must explain this and you must hurry."

"How can this be done?" Durell asked.

The old man told him. He coughed, and his voice faltered, and he shook like a tall old oak about to fall. Durell did not touch his proud figure. "They say it is impossible," the old man said. "I do not know how you can get in. But you must try. There are wild horses, and—" He waved a thin, shaking hand. "Please. I must return to my wife. I have put her to bed. And may God help you all. It is not comprehensible how

God arranged for you to pay for the sins of all the others."

O'Malley looked savage. "You say it's impossible, but maybe you know a way—"

Durell checked him. "Come along. Pick up Bruno and Joey. We'll see what we can do."

Beyond the side of the mountain the old Norman castle brooded darkly in the moonlight. *Sangieri,* Durell thought. Its square towers and strange Arab crenellations and airy arches floated beyond a steep gorge over which a narrow bridge led the way. Two men lounged against the stone wall near the bridge. A sentry box stood at the other end of the span, and another man stood there. The glow of his cigarette was like a firefly in the windy night.

Durell wondered how many others Kronin had to guard Zio against intrusions. He had Gabriella and his three sinners to put against an armed fortress. It seemed hopeless. But he could only take one step at a time. If he delayed to call for militia or the carabinieri, the birds would fly the coop, warned by other Brothers who undoubtedly had infiltrated the local law. They would only betray themselves by such an appeal.

To cross the bridge was only the first hurdle. "Frank?" he whispered. "We'll take the wall."

"I know what to do. The Congs in Vietnam were better in a place like this."

The guards were alert, but the long wait had blunted their senses. Durell ran in a crouch behind the stone fence that curved toward the bridge over the gorge. O'Malley flitted to the other side. The sound of the stream rushing far below covered any noise they made. O'Malley showed his jungle tactics well. They timed their attack together, and in ten seconds the two guards were down. Durell chopped at the throat of his man, then looked at O'Malley across the open end of the bridge. O'Malley crouched like a beast of prey over the prone figure of his target.

Then Durell saw the chain. It stretched across the span with small bells attached, to warn the guard at the sentry box fifty feet away. A heavy padlock prevented them from lowering it.

"Call Bruno," Durell whispered.

Bruno, Milan, and the girl came up behind the wall. Durell signaled the huge wrestler what had to be done. "It's rusted," he said. "Try to break it."

"Like it's paper," the big man rumbled.

"Be careful. Don't ring the bells."

Brutelli's strength was enormous and controlled. He felt carefully along the links until he found one that was more rusted than the others, then closed powerful hands on the old iron and twisted slowly. For some seconds it resisted him. His big face convulsed. The guard across the bridge threw away his cigarette; it arched far down into the stream at the bottom of the gorge. Then the guard stepped into the sentry box and was out of sight.

"Now!" Durell whispered.

Bruno grunted. There came a grinding click, another click as he bent the iron backward, and the chain snapped.

Durell caught one free end and lowered it with care to prevent the little bells from ringing. "All right. Joey?"

"Check."

The jockey ran across the bridge like an alert chipmunk. The guard was stepping from his box when Joey hit him. A moment later they were all across, carefully stepping over the sentry's sprawled figure.

"Now what?" O'Malley demanded.

"We've only just begun," Durell said.

"Let's leave Gabriella here until we get in."

"No, we may need her."

They were a team, Durell thought, precisely coordinated. He wondered wryly what General McFee, back at K Section in Washington, would think if he could see his sinners in action. Then he concentrated on the problem of getting into the fortress that loomed ahead.

It seemed impossible.

There was a sweep of moonlit lawn, a row of cypress bending in the mountain wind. Not a light shone; not a human was in sight. Durell signaled the others, and they circled wide behind the approach. The castle occupied a site on top of the dome of pasture and stone that commanded a view for miles around. It was a barren prospect. But the centuries since it had been a powerful medieval fortress had wrought changes. The old moat was filled in. On the north side there were small huts, fences and paddocks, a stone barn, and storage cribs. Durell and his companions filtered from one shadow to the next as they worked their way around to the back. Twice they had to halt while a patrolling guard passed.

O'Malley trembled like a hunting hound on leash. His tigerish eyes gleamed in the moonlight. "Two gets you five the old man is dead."

"Then we're finished. He's the only one who can give orders to keep Gabriella alive and the only one to give certain other orders I want given."

"To wipe out the sabotage network?"

Durell nodded, and O'Malley said, "But maybe he's for it. He took Kronin in, didn't he?"

"We'll answer that when we see Zio."

The fortress walls were lower on this side. There was a wide wooden gate that did not yield an inch, even when Bruno put his massive weight against it. From behind the gate came a sudden neighing sound.

"Uccelatti mentioned horses," O'Malley said.

Durell nodded again. "Joey?"

"I can't climb it," Milan said.

"Gabriella?"

"Yes, I can do it. My years in the circus—"

"Go ahead. Up and over."

"Now, wait, Cajun—" O'Malley objected.

"Shut up. We need all the special talent we have," Durell said.

He made a stirrup of his hands and gave the girl a quick boost. She was like a small, lithe cat, scrambling up the stone wall with quick, sure grips, and in a moment she disappeared on the other side. Then there came the thunder of angry hooves, another wild neighing like a trumpet blast, and the muffled sound of the girl dropping to the other side of the gate.

Muscles twitched in Joey Milan's face. "That horse is a nut. A kook. I know that sound. I been around horse farms long enough to recognize it. He'll kill her."

"You mean a wild stallion?" O'Malley asked thinly.

"No, no." Joey spoke with authority. "You get a wild horse, he's really as timid as a deer. They ain't like in the movies, Frankie. But you take one with his wires crossed, like he's been teased or just borned kookie, and you got trouble. They musta kept that one inside there just for somethin' like this, like a guard."

Suddenly the bars inside the gate rattled aside. Bruno heaved his weight against the massive portal and opened it enough for them all to slip through.

They almost met with disaster.

A huge black stallion reared and blotted out the moonlit sky with his enormous body and flashing hooves. His wild neighing shook the air. A hoof slammed down at Durell with a murderous blow, and he ducked aside. The gate shook as the heavy beast struck solid wood. Durell drew his gun.

"No, no!" Gabriella cried. "The poor thing—he is maddened, it is not natural, not his fault—"

Before he could check her, she slipped ahead with Joey Milan. They moved with perfect timing around the stallion, who backed, eyes rolling huge and wild. The great animal pawed the turf suspiciously. A light gleamed high in the black castle wall, and Durell thought he heard a man shout in alarm. Astonished, he watched the slight figure of the circus girl and the little jockey circle the enraged animal.

The stallion suddenly reared toward Gabriella; but with a single, lithe leap she was on his back. O'Malley swore in horror. Durell lifted his gun again and aimed at the animal's head, and Gabriella cried out, "No, Cajun! No!"

With her weight upon him, the stallion lost interest in the others. He bucked and reared, and it seemed as if Gabriella must surely be thrown and trampled under his hooves. Somehow she hung on. Joey Milan slipped like a shadow under the great, black animal and tried for his head, talking in soothing, rapid Italian, in a manner Durell had not heard him use before. The animal backed away, distracted, pawing restlessly. His tail swished high in the air. Gabriella's small fists remained tightly knotted in the animal's great mane. Her voice, too, was soft and lulling, like Joey's. The great horse suddenly shuddered, bucked, sunfished, and tried to turn and bite her. Joey scrambled out of the way, then darted in again. Step by step they edged the beast toward the stone stalls in the castle wall across the court. It was plain that the animal had been tormented or enraged, or perhaps simply allowed to develop a congenital feeling against people. But Gabriella and Joey were no strangers to horses. The great beast trembled, tossed his head, and backed into his stall. For another moment Gabriella clung to his broad back while Joey distracted him. Then, as smoothly as flowing water, she slid down and shut the stall door. At the same moment, Joey Milan slipped free.

The stallion was now safely penned.

O'Malley caught the running girl and held her in his arms. She laughed and said, "Oh, what a pity, such a beautiful horse!" She kissed him on the cheek and turned to Durell then. "Someone surely heard us and will look for us now."

"How much of this place can you remember?"

"I remember this place well now." Her long hair flowed over her shoulders, and her eyes gleamed with triumph. "What a magnificent animal! And Joey! Did you see him? Who would have thought he understood horses this way!"

More lights shone in the castle's windows. A man shouted. Durell heard the dim thud of distant feet.

"Gabriella, in which room did you have your interview with Zio? Can you recall that, too?"

"It was on the other side." She frowned in the gloom. "Near this place. We walked to a room that had windows that opened on a sheer cliff."

"The other side," Durell said. "Come on."

The courtyard was walled with high, delicate arches. They ran to a flagged parapet, turned right, and hugged the fortress wall. Gabriella's memory was correct. To the left, just beyond a ruined stone balustrade, was a sharp drop into the river gorge that looped around from the bridge. Durell paused to stare at the high wall of the ancient castle, which seemed to push them outward.

"Joey, was there any rope in the horse stalls?"

"I think so."

"Run back and get it."

While they waited Durell saw a buttress that had crumbled somewhat and offered footing a third of the way up. He pried loose a square block that was not too heavy, and when Joey returned with the rope, he tied the rock securely to the end of the line.

There was no alarm here yet. Durell clambered up the buttress, then heaved the rock and its attached line up and over the slanting roof tiles. His first attempt failed and the rock came down with the rope snaking after it. He tried again. This time it looped around an old chimney. He tugged hard, and it did not yield.

"All right, Gabriella. Up you go."

"What can we do on the roof?"

"It's our only way in."

They heard a distant, echoing shot. The guards were shooting at shadows. Durell turned sharply. "Bruno?"

"Yo."

"Lift her up as high as you can, for starters."

"Yo."

The girl went up easily, hand over hand, as if doing her tightrope act in the Vanini circus. O'Malley ground his teeth audibly. She paused, her body taut and leaning far out over the abyss as she braced her feet against the wall. Then she suddenly vanished over the eave, clinging for an instant to a gargoyle drain. A moment later she tugged at the rope as a signal for them to follow.

Bruno hesitated. "It won't hold me."

"Go ahead," Durell urged.

The big man climbed up laboriously, inch by inch. But he made it. Joey Milan went next, then O'Malley. The yelling and the wild shots came nearer now. Fortunately the roof was not as tightly pitched as it was in other parts of the building. Durell climbed up last. They stood together near the massive Norman chimney. The drop into the river gorge was dizzying.

"That way," Gabriella said, pointing.

Bruno rumbled, "I feel sick up here. I can't walk this roof."

"You've got to, you clod!" O'Malley snapped.

"I ain't no tightrope walker, Frankie."

"Hang on to my belt," Durell suggested.

The girl ran ahead, like a small cat, along the arch of the roof. At the end there was a narrow path of stone slabs atop a fine Moorish arch, built of stone the color of pale red wine. Some of the arches had crumbled, and there was a gap or two between the pediment slabs.

Bruno shuddered. "I'll never make it."

Durell said, "Tie the rope around him, O'Malley."

"I weigh too much. If I slip, I'll only pull all of you down with me."

"We'll take that chance."

It was slow, perilous going. Halfway across they paused and froze in the moonlight while armed men ran across the paving under the arches. If any had chanced to look up, they would have been as helpless as clay pigeons in a target gallery atop the pediment. But the hunters ran on out of sight.

At the end of the archway the castle roof was flat. There was a low stone coping and some pointed crenellations, which hid them from sight. Bruno gasped and sat down with relief.

"Now what?" O'Malley asked.

"This is the tower, the old keep of the castle," Gabriella explained. "The room where I saw Zio was in his personal apartment. There were stairs, I recall, but I don't see them now." She looked about, puzzled; her long hair was blown by the mountain wind. "The opening is gone."

Durell searched the stone floor of the tower roof. After a moment he found a square of cement that had been set into the roof flagstones. He pried at it with his fingers, but there was no grip on the heavy mass of concrete. It did not yield.

"Bruno?"

Bruno tried, too. Nothing happened. The big man grunted, heaved, sweated, and tugged. "It's sealed from the inside," he said.

"Then we go down the inner wall," Durell said.

There was a drop of three stories down the side of the tower to the next roof. Durell leaned over and studied it in the tricky moonlight. Gabriella flattened on her stomach beside him and looked down with him.

"That is Zio's window," she said.

It was fifteen feet below the edge of the roof. Too far to climb down. Durell got up. "The rope, Joey."

Milan looked stricken. "I left it tied to the chimney back there. I didn't think—"

More shouting came from below. The enemy had found the penned horses. Durell felt a desperate urgency. It was impossible to retreat along the top of the arches. They had come to the end of the way, trapped high above the complex, sprawling roofs.

Gabriella spoke suddenly. "Give me your trouser belts." She laughed elfishly at their startled faces. "I am a circus performer, remember? I have strong teeth for performing high-wire acts, hanging by my teeth—"

"No!" O'Malley exploded. "The belts won't be long enough. I won't let you. Besides, you use a special mouth bit, don't you?"

"I will use a buckle instead."

"You'll kill yourself," O'Malley said angrily.

She turned to Durell. "Cajun, I can and must get into that window. It won't be locked or barred at this height. Who could get into it? Kronin would not expect us this way. And Zio is in there. I know it."

"What about the rest of us, even if you make it?"

"I will find something, a hanging, a drapery, to toss up. You can follow me down that way."

164

Durell did not hesitate. They were lost if they stayed here much longer. "All right."

O'Malley sweated. "Cajun, you're crazy to let Gabriella try—"

"She's got to. Give me your belt."

He fastened them together, using Joey's and Bruno's as well, tested its strength, and gave the length of leather to Gabriella, who said quietly, "Bruno, you are the strongest, so you will hold the end."

"I'll be with him," Durell said.

She gave him the end of the belt at once. Then she took the end buckle in her mouth, tested it, and nodded. "Keep it tight at all times, please. You must keep me from striking the wall if I spin about, so you must extend your arms over the edge. I will need both hands to open the window, you see."

As she slid over the edge of the parapet O'Malley said thinly, "It's all my fault. I should never have gone to her and asked for help. If she falls, if anything happens to her—"

"Shut up," Durell said.

"Two gets you ten I don't walk out of here."

Durell looked at him sharply. "I thought you were worried about Gabriella, not yourself."

"I am. I'm going to see that she gets away all right, not matter what it costs. Two to ten. You'll see."

Gabriella lowered herself, and suddenly her weight came down hard on Durell's extended forearm. He lay flat on the roof, with Bruno beside him to steady his quivering muscles. Gabriella was small, but her long career with the Vaninis had given her a solid musculature. Her head was tossed back, and her teeth gleamed as she bit hard on the belt buckle. Her upturned face was white and strained. Her words were muffled as she spoke.

"Pay it out."

Bruno and Joey edged the leather between Durell's grip. Once they came to a smooth stretch of cowhide, and it started to slip, and the girl jolted downward a foot or two before they checked her. Her arms went out wide, and she spun like a small doll, her body

165

arched, her legs splayed for balance. It was a long way down. She lifted her arms and clung to the belt to steady herself for a heart-stopping moment, getting a better grip on the buckle with her teeth.

An eternity passed as they continued to ease her down to the level of the window.

There was a setback below the edge of the tower roof, and the window was perhaps two feet in from where Durell could look down. His wound was on fire with the pain and strain of supporting her weight. His body was bathed in cold sweat as Gabriella reached with both hands, hanging by her teeth, to explore the narrow casement. She spun away, whirling, and Durell felt the strain in his spine. Then she worked out again and checked herself with her hand on the frame. He could not see what she was doing under the lip of the parapet. Another eternity passed.

He heard a faint click.

She swung out, looking up. Her face was dead white, distorted by the mouth grip on the belt. Her arms waved. Far below, the cold stones waited for her if she fell.

She pushed herself farther out with one leg, then let her weight carry her in toward the window. There was a thin crash of breaking glass, a splintering of wood. She appeared again, a long cut showing on her cheek, the blood like a thin black ribbon across her mouth.

O'Malley cursed. Durell glanced at him. The man was crying. There came another wrenching swing, and the girl vanished, feet first.

The strain on the belt ended abruptly.

She was inside.

THEY followed one by one after she had thrown up
a long, knotted length of drapery, which Bruno fastened
to the parapet. Durell was the first down and he stood
still at the strange sight that met his eyes.

Everything in the big, square tower room was dark
and somber. The girl knelt beside a huge Spanish tester
bed with carved posts and a dusty red canopy embroider-
ed with tarnished gilt. There were heavy, carved chests,
tall straight-backed chairs with faded tapestry covers, a
wealth of dull gold in a shining candelabrum. A single
taper guttered beside the bed, where the girl knelt.

The smell of incredible age and illness filled the cold
stone room, like that of a musty crypt.

Gabriella was crying.

Propped up on dark pillows, the old man's face,
like death's head, turned to regard her. His shock of
white hair only added to the skeletal effect. She held
his long thin hand, which seemed transparent in the
candlelight, and kissed it and let her tears fall upon it.

"Zio, Zio," she murmured.

The old man watched in silence as Durell came near.
His wasted body scarcely made any shape at all under
the black coverlet. But the eyes were as alert as a
hawk's, still intelligent and wary with the caution of age
and adversity. Durell snapped a finger at Bruno, who
went to check the big oaken door. Bruno tested it,
found it locked and barred on the outside. Another door
led to a primitive bath. It was empty. There was no
other way out of the place. O'Malley hauled in the knotted drapery and closed the shattered casement window.
A floodlight struck the wall out there a moment later,

then passed on. Voices echoed curiously from the court-yard below. Joey Milan took up a post at the window. It was all done with speed and a fine economy of movement.

The old man's voice was thin but sure. "Who are these men, Gabriella?"

"Do you know me, then?" she whispered.

"I would know you at any time, my dearest." He spoke in pure, limpid Italian. "You have never been far from my thoughts for all these years, child. Are you well? And are you happy?"

"I am well, yes. But not happy."

"So you managed to come to me?"

"Yes. It was very difficult."

"You must forgive me. I was a foolish old man and I pay for my mistakes. All that I have done in my long years has now been wasted."

"No, Zio," she whispered.

"Are these men here to kill me?"

"They are my friends."

"I am waiting for someone to kill me."

"They have come to help." She spoke earnestly. "You promised to protect me all my life, Zio. And you have, you have. Whenever I was troubled, I needed only to think of you and I felt better, I was happy. Then these men told me that *you* needed my help, and I see it was true."

"Gabriella, my child. . . ."

"What have they done to you?" she whispered. "What did they dare do to Vecchio Zio?"

"I was old and foolish. All things pass. All life is transient. Hope and ambition and dreams—they go, as the days and the years fly by."

"You are still strong. Your name alone—"

"Others speak in my name now, Gabriella, while I am kept here like an old and dying animal."

"You are a lion," she said. "You will not die."

Durell approached the bed and stood beside the girl. He looked down gravely at the old face, the white mane of hair, the pale, intelligent eyes. Gently he lifted Gabriella's cheek from Zio's hand and drew her aside. Zio regarded him without fear, nodding a little. The candle sputtered and threw odd shadows in the room.

"We do not have much time, Zio," he said in gentle Italian. "They know we are here. Your guards—"

"They are not my people."

"How long have you been a prisoner here?"

"Time has no meaning. Days and weeks, to be sure. I do not know. They feed me and give me such medicine as I need. They wish to keep me alive, I think, since only in that way am I useful to them."

"I understand. They speak for you to the Fratelli. Is it Kronin? Is he here? You must tell me."

"Kronin is a devil. He is Satan come to pay me for my sins. But only his people come up here to see me."

"Then, some of the men who are hunting us now can be trusted if you appeared?"

"Perhaps. I do not know."

"Do you know what Kronin has been doing with your people? Do you know why we have come this long way to see you?"

Gabriella said quickly, "We could not believe it was you, dear Zio, who gave these terrible orders, who turned the honorable Fratelli into a tool for the enemies of our country and Mr. Durell's."

The old man's eyes closed for a moment. His mouth worked silently, and there was a faint movement under the coverlet as he sighed. "I see. Baron Uccelatti was mistaken to introduce that man Kronin to us. But the responsibility is mine. I am the chief. It is in my name that the men obey." The hawk's eyes opened and fixed Durell with a piercing stare. Anger overcame the regret and guilt he expressed. "Have they tried to harm Gabriella, to keep her from coming here?"

"They tried to kill her," Durell said.

"And you saved her?"

"I and these men with me."

"In America one thinks of the Fratelli as criminals. But we are not meant to be that. There is much to be done for our people in Sicily. We are not bandits, although history once forced us to be." The old man paused. "Ah, well. It is not important now."

"It is important," Durell said, "that you be released so you can appear to your people who are loyal to you and correct the damage that Kronin has done by giving orders in your name."

"It is impossible."

"We are here and we were told it would be impossible to get here."

"But you cannot escape now."

"We must try," Durell said urgently.

"Very well," Zio said. "Help me out of bed."

O'Malley said, "They're coming up, Cajun. They know we're here."

Footsteps pounded on the stone stairs beyond the barred oaken door. Someone shouted an order, and Durell recognized Kronin's voice with a cold flood of rage along his nerves. The girl helped Zio out of bed and into his clothes, which she had secured from a massive wardrobe cabinet. O'Malley swore softly. His pale eyes were wide and held a peculiar, farseeing look.

"We're mice in a trap, Cajun."

"Bruno? Can you handle the door?"

"Bust it, you mean?" the big man asked.

"When I tell you to."

"Yo."

"Gabriella, get out of the line of fire. Take Zio into the bathroom."

"But you and O'Malley—"

"Do as I say. Joey, keep your gun ready."

The little man nodded. The footsteps pounded up the steps again, then paused. Then there was a scraping sound. For several seconds no one breathed.

"Kronin!" Durell called.

There was a harsh laugh from the other side of the panel. "You have done my work well for me, Durell! You are exactly where I wanted to get you!"

"Now, Bruno," Durell said quietly.

The big man backed up two steps and then hurled himself at the heavy planking. The door, for all its apparent solidity, was old and worm-eaten. There came a splintering crash, the squeal of old and rusty bolts

170

torn from the strap hinges. Bruno fell to his knees, his face anguished as the big door fell outward. He grabbed at his shoulder. "I busted it!"

But Durell did not hear. Light slammed into the room with almost physical force from beyond the broken doorway. Over Bruno's huge bulk he saw Karl Kronin, tall and vulturine, his face startled. Behind him were two men in dark business suits. They were Chinese. All three were armed with machine pistols.

What followed came too fast to control. As the door smashed down and Bruno fell, Durell fired over him. The shot was thunderous in the stone stairwell. Because of Bruno, he missed Kronin, but one of the Chinese fell backward down the stairs, his machine-pistol ripping a long blast of fire that stitched the air above Durell's head. At that moment Gabriella came out of the bathroom with Zio. Kronin's eyes widened, and his shot was aimed at either the girl or the old man—Durell was never sure which. O'Malley intervened. He cried out something in the confusion of rapid gunfire and leaped over Bruno's big body, and Durell saw Kronin's bullet smash into O'Malley's body. Durell jumped, caught Kronin as the bald man swung about, struck at Kronin's throat, struck again. There could be only one answer to this moment. One of them had to die. It had been a long time coming. Kronin's grin was fixed and unnatural. He stepped back, staggering, as Durell tried to free his own weapon in the close quarters of the stairwell. Kronin's metal leg came up in a savage kick that sent shocking pain up through Durell's belly. They grappled, slammed against the iron railing. Kronin gasped as Durell drove his forearm across the man's throat; then a grin of triumph widened his mouth as he brought up his metal knee. But Durell knew of the weapon concealed there now. He caught the man's leg, heaved, and drove his weight against Kronin's upper body. Abruptly Kronin went over the rail. Durell caught himself just in time to keep from going after him. He clung to the iron webbing with his last strength, watching Kronin fall the long distance down to the stone floor

171

below. The body bounced once, and then didn't move. Kronin's neck and back looked broken.

Turning, he saw that the second Chinese had flung down his gun, and Durell knocked up Milan's weapon as Joey started to shoot him. "We'll need that one," Durell said hoarsely.

It had all taken less than ten seconds.

Silence drifted back in the room. He straightened slowly. He looked at Gabriella and felt a great weight descend upon him, a thick exhaustion, and a sense of loss.

"Are you all right?"

Her mouth shook. "Yes. But O'Malley—"

"Zio?"

"Yes," said the old man.

"Then let's go down and hear you give orders to your men. You're the chief again."

The girl cried out, "But O'Malley is—!"

Durell checked her and went down first. His wounded shoulder was bleeding again. He felt as if he had been struck across the stomach with the flat of a board. Every step hurt. Bruno followed him slowly, and Joey Milan kept the surviving Chinese under guard. The Chinese was sputtering something about diplomatic rights, but Durell paid no attention. He took Gabriella's hand and forced her to go down with him.

Kronin was dead. It would be a relief, Durell thought dimly, to close that file, at last. . . .

Zio took command in a matter of minutes. As soon as he could, Durell went back up the stairs to look at O'Malley. There were bullet holes in O'Malley's chest, and it was a miracle the man still breathed. He knelt beside his boyhood friend and touched O'Malley's throat for a pulse, and O'Malley opened his pale eyes. They looked dreamy, staring at something far, far away.

"Cajun?"

"I'm here, Frank."

"Is Gabriella—?"

"She's all right. Not hurt, thanks to you."

"I made—a lot of mistakes—but not that one."

"It's all over now."

172

"All my fault, though—I didn't think—when I cut out on you in Naples—"

Gabriella stared at the dying man with wide, dry eyes. A group of armed men came running back up the stairs to the tower. A sharp order from Zio checked them. They stared at the old man and lowered their arms. O'Malley coughed, and blood gushed over his lower lip.

"Cajun, remember the time—we were kids—remember how it was—"

"I remember, O'Malley."

"Take Gabriella—with you—"

"Yes."

O'Malley looked at the girl and tried to give her his old reckless grin.

A moment later Durell bent and picked him up in his arms and walked out into the moonlit night. Gabriella followed silently.

"I'll take you home, Gabriella, as he asked," Durell said. He looked down at the burden he carried. "I'll take O'Malley, too."

HE BURIED O'Malley in Rome. O'Malley had no family, no relatives anywhere. It seemed the best thing to do. The sun shone with gentle warmth as Durell and Gabriella, the only mourners, left the cemetery. The girl had worn a simple black dress for the ceremony and still had not wept. She had spoken little on the flight from Palermo, and Durell had not pressed for her future plans.

In Rome he used the K Section Central facilities to dictate a report to Thompson, in Geneva, and a relay message to London and Washington. Thompson told him that Colonel Mignon's and Amos Rand's deaths in Switzerland had been explained to Swiss Security. There would be no publicity. Kronin's sabotage plans and the lists of Kronin's men planted in the Fratelli della Notte were in the hands of the F.B.I. The saboteurs were being rounded up. K Section was letting the Bureau take credit for the sweep.

Thompson had flown down from Geneva that day. He looked wryly amused as he read Durell's reports.

"A pity about O'Malley. What about the other two—ah—sinners? Mr. Brutelli and Mr. Milan—"

"Bruno's shoulder will mend," Durell told him. "He decided to stay in Palermo. He likes the food there."

"And Joey Milan?"

"He'll work for Zio. He can get a jockey's license in Sicily, but he said he wanted to work with Zio's horses. Breeding them for the track and so forth. I doubt if we'll see either man again. And McElroy is squaring things with the Italian authorities."

Thompson cleared his throat. "I'm sorry about O'Malley, really."

"It happened," Durell said. "He did what he thought he had to do. We owe him a great deal."

"And the girl?"

"I don't know what to do about her yet."

"Awkward," Thompson said. "You see, I've gotten leave from Washington to return Deirdre Padgett to Rome. Just so you could have a few days with her before you go back to report to Dickinson McFee. Deirdre is your—ah—?"

"My girl, yes," Durell said.

"Well, I'm sure you can handle it. She'll arrive tonight. Leonardo da Vinci Airport, Flight two-one-two."

"That's fine," Durell said. "It will help."

From the cemetery where he had buried O'Malley he took a taxi with Gabriella to the Borghese Gardens and walked with her under the trees and across the quiet lawns. Children played, nurses pushed perambulators, and traffic hummed along the curving drives. The sky was warm and cloudless. Gabriella walked half a pace ahead of him, her blonde head bowed slightly. Durell told her about Deirdre, speaking quietly, and how he planned to meet her at the airport that evening. Gabriella listened in pale silence as he explained how very special Deirdre was to him.

"We've been apart for some time," he said. "I've missed her very much."

Gabriella said nothing. But he could not let her long silence go on. He touched her arm as they walked together through the green park. "Gabriella?"

She looked up at him, her face small and piquant. "What is it, Sam?"

"I understand how you felt about O'Malley—"

"But you do *not* understand. I thought—I am not experienced in such things. I thought I loved him. He was strange to me, and exciting, and—different from all I had ever known. But I know now that I did not love him. His life could never be mine, you see."

"Then why didn't you stay with Zio?"

"That is not my life, either. It is time I stopped being a little girl about all that, is it not?"

"Then what will you do?"

She turned to face him, standing on the garden walk, her body small and slim and straight in the dappled sunlight that sifted down like golden dust through the tall trees. Traffic hummed from a drive nearby. Birds called in the shrubbery. It was difficult to believe they were in the heart of Rome. She smiled and reached up to touch his face. Then suddenly she laughed and hugged him and buried her face against his chest. Abruptly she drew back with a small sound of self-reproach.

"I am sorry. I forgot. You are recovering from a wound in your shoulder."

"It's much better now."

"Sam, you must not worry about me. I know you love this girl, this Deirdre, who is coming to Rome to-night. It is all right. For a time, it is true, I thought I was in love with you, myself. But—" She shook her head and smiled again. "I am going home, Sam."

"Where is that?"

"The Vanini circus, of course. That is where I belong. That is the life I know and love. I shall go back there and wait—wait for life to touch me again. The next time I shall know better what to do."

Durell stared down gravely into her eyes. Then he nodded and took her hand, and they walked together to find a taxi.

Get 2 Free Books,

Plus 2 Free Gifts—

Love Inspired HISTORICAL

just for trying the Reader Service!

YES! Please send me 2 FREE Love Inspired® Historical novels and my 2 FREE mystery gifts (gifts are worth about $10 retail). After receiving them, if I don't wish to receive any more books, I can return the shipping statement marked "cancel." If I don't cancel, I will receive 4 brand-new novels every month and be billed just $5.24 per book in the U.S. or $5.74 per book in Canada. That's a savings of at least 13% off the cover price. It's quite a bargain! Shipping and handling is just 50¢ per book in the U.S. and 75¢ per book in Canada.* I understand that accepting the 2 free books and gifts places me under no obligation to buy anything. I can always return a shipment and cancel at any time. The free books and gifts are mine to keep no matter what I decide.

102/302 IDN GLWZ

Name	(PLEASE PRINT)	
Address		Apt. #
City	State/Prov.	Zip/Postal Code

Signature (if under 18, a parent or guardian must sign)

Mail to the **Reader Service:**
IN U.S.A.: P.O. Box 1341, Buffalo, NY 14240-8531
IN CANADA: P.O. Box 603, Fort Erie, Ontario L2A 5X3

Want to try two free books from another series?
Call 1-800-873-8635 or visit www.ReaderService.com.

* Terms and prices subject to change without notice. Prices do not include applicable taxes. Sales tax applicable in N.Y. Canadian residents will be charged applicable taxes. Offer not valid in Quebec. This offer is limited to one order per household. Books received may not be as shown. Not valid for current subscribers to Love Inspired Historical books. All orders subject to approval. Credit or debit balances in a customer's account(s) may be offset by any other outstanding balance owed by or to the customer. Please allow 4 to 6 weeks for delivery. Offer available while quantities last.

Your Privacy—The Reader Service is committed to protecting your privacy. Our Privacy Policy is available online at www.ReaderService.com or upon request from the Reader Service.

We make a portion of our mailing list available to reputable third parties that offer products we believe may interest you. If you prefer that we not exchange your name with third parties, or if you wish to clarify or modify your communication preferences, please visit us at www.ReaderService.com/consumerschoice or write to us at Reader Service Preference Service, P.O. Box 9062, Buffalo, NY 14240-9062. Include your complete name and address.

LIHI7R2

Get 2 Free Books,
Plus 2 Free Gifts—
just for trying the Reader Service!

HARLEQUIN

HEARTWARMING™

YES! Please send me 2 FREE Harlequin® Heartwarming™ Larger-Print novels and my 2 FREE mystery gifts (gifts worth about $10 retail). After receiving them, if I don't wish to receive any more books, I can return the shipping statement marked "cancel." If I don't cancel, I will receive 4 brand-new larger-print novels every month and be billed just $5.49 per book in the U.S. or $6.24 per book in Canada. That's a savings of at least 19% off the cover price. It's quite a bargain! Shipping and handling is just 50¢ per book in the U.S. and 75¢ per book in Canada.* I understand that accepting the 2 free books and gifts places me under no obligation to buy anything. I can always return a shipment and cancel at any time. The free books and gifts are mine to keep no matter what I decide.

161/361 IDN GLWT

Name	(PLEASE PRINT)
Address	Apt. #
City	State/Prov.	Zip/Postal Code

Signature (if under 18, a parent or guardian must sign)

Mail to the **Reader Service:**
IN U.S.A.: P.O. Box 1341, Buffalo, NY 14240-8531
IN CANADA: P.O. Box 603, Fort Erie, Ontario L2A 5X3

Want to try two free books from another line?
Call 1-800-873-8635 today or visit www.ReaderService.com.

* Terms and prices subject to change without notice. Prices do not include applicable taxes. Sales tax applicable in N.Y. Canadian residents will be charged applicable taxes. Offer not valid in Quebec. This offer is limited to one order per household. Books received may not be as shown. Not valid for current subscribers to Harlequin Heartwarming Larger-Print books. All orders subject to approval. Credit or debit balances in a customer's account(s) may be offset by any other outstanding balance owed by or to the customer. Please allow 4 to 6 weeks for delivery. Offer available while quantities last.

HW17R

READERSERVICE.COM

Manage your account online!

- Review your order history
- Manage your payments
- Update your address

> ### We've designed the Reader Service website just for you.

Enjoy all the features!

- Discover new series available to you, and read excerpts from any series.
- Respond to mailings and special monthly offers.
- Browse the Bonus Bucks catalog and online-only exculsives.
- Share your feedback.

Visit us at:
ReaderService.com

RS16R